Praise for
THE SURPRISING PLACE

"Malinda McCollum's linked short stories work like small bombs in the consciousness. She understands American optimism enough to turn it on its head, creating scenes with darkness enough to make Eudora Welty and Flannery O'Connor proud. Her understanding of the anti-heroine burns across a landscape McCollum knows well. Come prepared. You may find stories such as 'The Fifth Wall' as unforgettable as any by Denis Johnson or Christine Schutt. While the degradation arrives quick and dirty, its question lingers: How much can the pursuit of happiness vacate a person?"

—Edie Meidav, Juniper Prize for Fiction judge and author of *Kingdom of the Young*

"Malinda McCollum does sinister like no one since Robert Stone. Her stories are . . . populated with hopeless and hapless characters who are both compelling and surprisingly loveable. The Surprising Place will leave you stunned."

—Mark Jude Poirier, author of *Goats and Modern Ranch Living*

THE SURPRISING PLACE

THE SURPRISING PLACE

Stories

Malinda McCollum

UNIVERSITY OF MASSACHUSETTS PRESS
Amherst and Boston

Printed in the United States of America

ISBN 978-1-62534-348-2 (paper)

Designed by Sally Nichols
Set in Adobe Garamond Pro and Treadstone
Printed and bound by Maple Press, Inc.

Cover design by Kristina Kachele Design llc

Library of Congress Cataloging-in-Publication Data
A catalog record for this book is available from the Library of Congress.

British Library Cataloguing-in-Publication Data
A catalog record for this book is available from the British Library.

Grateful acknowledgment is made to the following publications in which versions of these stories originally appeared: "He Ain't Jesus," "Sharks," and "Us, Crazy" in *Epoch;* "Good Monks" in *McSweeney's;* "Think Straight" in *StoryQuarterly;* "The Fifth Wall" in the *Paris Review;* and "Kicks" in *Zyzzyva.* In addition, "The Fifth Wall" appears in the anthology *The Paris Review Book of People with Problems.* "He Ain't Jesus" appears in the anthology *The Pushcart Prize XXVIII: Best of the Small Presses,* edited by Bill Henderson. "Good Monks" appears in the anthology *The Worst Years of Your Life: Stories for the Geeked-Out, Angst-Ridden, Lust-Addled, and Deeply Misunderstood Adolescent in All of Us,* edited by Mark Jude Poirier.

For my parents, Kay and Tom

CONTENTS

ACKNOWLEDGMENTS

Thanks to the editors of the publications in which many of these stories first appeared—particularly Eli Horowitz, Ben Ryder Howe, Brigid Hughes, Howard Junker, and Michael Koch—and to my agent, Jennifer Carlson, for her exceptional patience and kindness. Thanks also to Courtney Andree, Mary Dougherty, and Sally Nichols at the University of Massachusetts Press and to Edie Meidav and Sheryl Johnston for their support of this book.

For their guidance and encouragement, I thank John Barth, Stephen Dixon, John L'Heureux, D. R. MacDonald, Jean McGarry, James Alan McPherson, Reginald McKnight, Susan Power, Marilynne Robinson, Gilbert Sorrentino, Robert Stone, Elizabeth Tallent, and Tobias Wolff.

For their acumen and inspiration, I thank Andrea Bewick, Amber Dermont, Doug Dorst, Jordan Ellenberg, Nathan Englander,

ACKNOWLEDGMENTS

Adam Johnson, Ben Neihart, Ron Nyren, Daniel Orozco, Julie Orringer, ZZ Packer, Angela Pneuman, Mark Poirier, Ed Schwarzchild, and Ann Joslin Williams.

I'm forever grateful to my parents, Kay and Tom McCollum, for their stories and spirits. Thanks to my sister, Melissa, and my brother, Tom, for their generosity and insight. Thanks to my husband, Tony Varallo, for walking this long path with me. And thanks to my children, Gus and Ruby, for everything.

THE SURPRISING PLACE

HE AIN'T JESUS

Green bought the one-room bank building on the outskirts of Des Moines for himself. An air mattress inflated in the vault, a candle in a jar of sand, and all that was left was to pick up a girl and a few bottles. In the morning, sun came through the bank door's ox-eye window and made him and the girl and the room red and holy. No, he thought, taking it all in, nobody knew everything about him yet.

He dropped off the girl and went home to his wife in town. Nora was sitting with his brother, Roy, at the kitchen table, biting toast and drinking coffee. The sight of them filled him with a rage both oversized and misdirected, but he didn't resist it. These days he'd follow anything to wherever it led.

"And?" Nora said when she saw him.

"First this one unexpected thing happened," he said. "And

then another thing, and before you knew it, boom, it's dawn." He poured himself a cup of coffee from the percolator on the counter. "Plus traffic."

His wife picked up her cup and walked by Green, spilling coffee onto his shoe. She made it to the living room before he heard her begin to cry.

"A single lie is more convincing than a lot all at once," Roy said. "Asshole." He took hold of his brace, straightened his leg, and stood. He was younger than Green, but looked older, hair fine and thinning, nose copper, eyes set low in his face.

"There are enough good times in the world for us both," Green said. "No need to be jealous and call me mean names."

"So you're flying high," said Roy. "Well, here's something to bring you down. Butcher's skipped on his rent again."

A year earlier, the brothers had broken into real estate with a small profit from their engraving business. They assumed a loan on a house, and Green found a tenant who rented with the option to buy. Mat Butcher was a self-employed contractor, and in the summer, things were fine. But in the winter, his jobs disappeared, and now he hadn't paid rent in three months.

"He's playing," Roy continued. "We need to boot him."

"Five kids," Green said. "I'm no sap, but he's got five kids and winter's here. Where's he going to go?"

"His daddy's a minister in town. Let the little lamb wander home."

Green agreed to talk to Butcher. But he went to Nora first. He sat beside her on the couch, and she let him dry her face with his thumbs.

"I was out all night hunting for teeth," he said, attempting fancy. "A dead person's teeth are a powerful ingredient in a potion for love."

"You hate me," she said. "How did I end up with a person who hates me? I always thought I loved myself better than that."

"I'm here now."

"Funny," she said. "I don't believe you."

His fingers were still on her face. He studied them. "I love you."

"Lucky me," she said.

He wished she could see herself, how good she looked angry, eyes darker, skin righteous and red. He said, softly, "We've got time."

"Super," she said. "It's not over."

"It was a bad night." He took his hands away. "No more, no less."

"Here's what I want to ask," she said and leaned forward, her contempt coming at him like a fist. "Do you ever get the urge to talk to me like a real person?"

He shouldn't have, but he made his face blank. "Real person?" he said. "Where's one of those?"

The house they rented to Butcher had a simple façade marred only by a strip of ornate fretwork—completely unsuited to the house—a previous owner had carved badly and attached above the front door with nails. The same owner had replaced the house's serviceable concrete sidewalk with large fieldstones sunk into the lawn in an irregular path. The path had been recently shoveled, and Green stepped over it surely. Standing on the porch, he could see the house's double-hung windows were lined, on the inside, with foil.

"I'm remodeling," Butcher said, opening the door. Since Green's last visit, Butcher had grown a soft dark mustache that nearly hid the tension in his lips. His skin was as pebbly as an avocado's.

Green stepped through the door. Inside, pale light everywhere teased him. Dust hung in the air. A ladder up against the far wall rose to a top floor window. But the top floor itself had disappeared.

"Yeah," Green said, blinking. "I remember when this was a two-story house."

"More like one and a half, with those slanted ceilings." Butcher pointed to the low-pitched gable roof. "I couldn't abide that short little half-story. So I decided to lower the floor, to have more headroom up top. Had to tear out the staircase to do that. Had to tear out the existing floor."

The house looked useless. For the first time in a long time, Green realized the importance of ceilings and walls.

"I have to say the house this way has its own kind of charm," Butcher said. "Like a big church. You know my daddy's a minister?"

Green walked through the house's first, and now only, floor. Gray chunks of plaster rested on the ground like geodes. It was so cold his breath condensed into steam when he asked, "Where's he preach?"

"You're not going to call the cops are you?" Butcher had moved into the small kitchen, next to the stove, one hand on the unlit range.

"You think I should?"

"Naw, of course not. Hey, help yourself to a beer." He waved to the refrigerator.

Green joined him and removed a beer from the refrigerator's dark and lonely interior. "How long do you think this remodeling is going to take?" he asked carefully, sipping.

"Well, I started the job, but now with winter I'm not working. I don't have the cash to get what I need to finish. And that's where my trouble lies."

But there was no trouble in his voice. The lack of it made Green nervous. He took another drink. "Mat," he said, "you're already behind on the rent. We've cut you a break these last few months, and I know you got a wife and all these kids."

"Wife's gone." Butcher cleared his throat. "I thought, when I married her, that she was a Proverbs 31 type girl. But then I came to find out there wasn't much Bible about her." He touched his eyes, then wiped his fingertips on his shirt. "Anyway, I'm doing this work for free. I hope you'll put that into consideration when I exercise my option to buy. Maybe work the price a little."

"Where's your daddy preach?" Green asked again. "Somewhere in town?"

"Look here," Butcher said. "Let me speak clearly now. Do you always get what you pray for?"

The abrupt switch required of Green just one moment. Then he thought of the things he prayed for: small steps toward wisdom, occasional moments of serenity, effortless achievement and fame.

"I guess I don't," he said.

"Does that mean God's a liar? He's selling you a bill of goods?"

Green realized it was the kind of conversation in which he was supposed to be silent and let the other person expound.

"No, God answers your prayers. But it's not like going into the grocery store, picking out your bananas, taking them up to the stand. Praying's like casting a seed. You sow it, then you wait. It blooms on down the line. But you got to wait first."

"You're telling me I need to wait?"

"I'm telling you to sow the seed. Prime the pump, my man. Then you can wait."

There was an expansiveness about Butcher that Green suddenly suspected arose from some outside source. "Are you on something?" he asked Butcher. "What exactly are you taking?"

Butcher laughed, then came over and laid his hands on Green's shoulders. His breath smelled like gasoline. "There is what I'm supposed to be taking," he announced, "and then there is what I do, in fact, take."

Green nodded and shrugged off Butcher's hands. He could see it. Inside that gap, things might be revealed.

From another place in the house a child moaned. Green followed Butcher into the living room. Homemade toys were scattered throughout the room—socks with buttons stitched on to make puppets, pieces of wood sanded into smooth shapes. Three kids slept on a plaid sleeping bag unzipped in front of the fire. The littlest one wore fuzzy pajamas and a pair of Moon Boots.

"You're dying to wake them up, aren't you?" Butcher said, voice low and fond. "Sometimes I have a hard time letting them sleep." He walked over to the littlest child and nudged her sweetly with his foot.

"Hold on," Green said. "Don't go and wake her up for me."

"For you?" Butcher laughed as the little girl made a small noise and stretched her arms. "You think this is for you?" He lifted the girl and swung her through the air like a sack of flour.

Green started his car three times before the engine took hold. He watched Butcher's house diminish in the rearview mirror and then turned his attention to the snow-crusted roads leading home. When he passed the drive-through Chinese restaurant on Merle Hay, he made a left turn and headed back. A line of cars waited, engines running, alongside the pink building overhung with a billboard that read EGG ROLLS AND MILKSHAKES DONE RIGHT HERE. Green pulled into the line. When he advanced to the speaker and placed his order, he sensed in the voice that responded a boundless hostility, the very thing he was attempting, temporarily, to avoid. Was his complicity in all things fucked-up that apparent? Could people hear it in his voice? He drove home, melancholy, a bag of egg rolls warm in his lap.

Ray and Molly and Nora were in the basement, working on a big trophy order for a men's club on the south side. There was another order to engrave a message on the inside of a wedding band, but they saved expensive items like that for Green because—and it was a surprise to all of them—he had the steadiest hand. Nora set type the fastest, and that's what she was doing, laying new letters into the tray after Roy finished engraving each nameplate with the double-armed engraver. Molly sat at the end of the line, assembling the trophies, screwing tennis players onto marble bases and then attaching nameplates to the bases with two-sided tape.

Roy had started engraving in high school when their father thought it would be a good way to make money without straining his polio-stricken leg. He bought Roy an engraving machine, and Roy built up a small business doing trophies and plaques. Later he brought in Green and, eventually, their wives, who assumed more responsibility as the brothers made their foray into real estate. In addition to the house they rented to Butcher, they had purchased an apartment complex called the Coronado, the management of which consisted mostly of repair work on the building's washing machines, which tenants jammed with wooden tokens that were almost quarter-sized.

Green set the bag of egg rolls on the ping pong table in the center of the room. Roy and Molly and Nora stopped working and gathered around the food.

"What did Butcher say?" Roy asked, untying the bag.

"He was giving me lots of Bible talk. I think he's sunk way in."

"Remember that time I picked up his check last summer?" Molly said. She spoke in a high whispery voice that Green tried to resist but couldn't. "He told me weak-wombed women can conceive, but can't bring forth a child."

"He was talking about your womb?" Roy said.

Nora didn't say anything. She carefully unpeeled an egg roll, picking out slivers of mushrooms and pork. Green watched her. What else could he do?

"He told me I needed to sow some seeds," Green said. "Sow seeds and then sit around and wait."

Nora snorted. "He sounds like a wise man. Next time you meet one of those, take advantage of it and ask him a question." She flicked a piece of meat at Green.

He decided to ignore her. "You know Butcher plans to buy the house," he said. "But he wanted the second story to have more headroom. He's ripped out the second floor so he can rebuild it lower. But now he's run out of money."

Roy let his egg roll fall to the table. "He's gutting the house?"

"I figure it this way. We want to get the house back in shape, whether he buys it or not. Our best option is to give him the money for materials to finish the work."

"You're so soft." Roy shook his head.

"A marshmallow," Nora said. "A mouse."

"Our other option is to evict him and hire a contractor to fix everything. Then we have to pay for materials and labor, which is where the real money comes in."

"I never should have let you talk to him," Roy said. "You don't know people. You don't know who's who."

"His wife left him and he has five children. We have a wrecked house. I don't know what else we can do."

"You don't know now," Nora said, "but you'll learn." Molly sighed and covered Nora's hand with her own.

Sometimes her bitterness impaired him. But he wouldn't let it tonight. Buoyed by a sudden swell of self-regard, he found the wedding ring in the file cabinet where orders were stored. The ring was a simple gold band that fit easily into the vise beneath the double-armed engraver. He made the necessary adjustments to the machine and laid a line of Italianate type in the tray. Taking a tool in each hand, he first set the tracer to the grooves of the types and then the engraver to the ring. Only then did he catch the room's mood, the uprising of ill will. They were hoping he'd ruin the ring, even though they'd have to replace it, even though the jewelry store would never use them again.

Well, he knew his role was to disappoint. He engraved the letters into the band, unfastened the ring, and held it to the light. It was perfect.

"*A greater love hath no man,*" he read.

"Fuck you," Nora said.

Green established an account for Butcher at the lumberyard, with a limit. A few days later, the lumberyard called to say the limit was reached and Butcher was trying to charge more. The clerk put Butcher on the phone, and Green agreed to meet him at the house. When he arrived, Green could see the difference immediately. The partition that had shielded the kitchen from the dining room had been torn down. In the dining room, the carpeting had been untacked, and much of the flooring was pulled up, leaving beams exposed. Green half-expected to see flowers growing wild through the floor.

Butcher took his arm quickly and led him into the living room, which was empty of furniture. Two of his kids slept on blankets in front of the fire, and Butcher lifted one of them onto his lap to make room for Green.

"Let me tell you the truth," Butcher said right away. "Most of the stuff I bought from that yard is gone. I resold it discounted to friends so I could buy my kids food."

"I'm not proud of it," he continued, "but listen to this. See that over there?" He pointed to a ladder leading to a high window. "The other night I climbed that ladder and spent a long time looking out. Not up at the sky either. Down, at the ground."

The kid in his lap exhaled happily.

"I opened the window. I took off my shirt—I can't remember why I did that—then I leaned out the window. I thought about doing it. I really did."

"That's a fixed window," Green told him.

"How do you mean?"

"It doesn't open."

Butcher stared with a face full of wonder. "Do you think I'm lying?" he asked. "Do you think I'm not in a bad way?"

For a moment, Green attempted to imagine the house as Butcher imagined it. Instead, he had a vision of his own future, laid out neat. There were no surprises waiting for him. The heady life he'd once hoped for was a joke.

"You're going to have to leave," he said.

"Hold on," said Butcher. "You're losing me." Clutching the child, he stood slowly and left the room. When he returned, he carried the kid and a bottle of off-brand tequila. He handed the bottle to Green and then reassumed his position on the blanket.

"If you're not too busy this weekend, I'd like to invite you to my daddy's annual barbecue. He likes to do it in the dead of winter." Butcher broke into a slow, dirge-like song: "*In the bleak midwinter, when the lakes are stone . . .*" He stopped singing. "That man can flat out lay down some Q," he said.

"I'll come by this weekend," Green said, "and we'll talk about a moving plan."

"We'll talk," said Butcher. "Beyond that, who can know?"

Green passed the bottle. The boy in Butcher's lap turned over. When the fire flared up, he could see the boy had a black eye.

"What happened?" he asked.

Butcher sighed. "I always tell him, never attack anybody. Only strike if you're struck first. Well, these boys jumped him. He started swinging. He's a good kid, but he ain't Jesus, if you know what I mean."

"I know what you mean," Green said, though he didn't.

Butcher lifted the boy and gave him a gentle shake before standing him on his feet. "You've got a club in your hand," he cooed. "You'll tear up anything that gets in your way."

The child, dozy, stumbled to Green and climbed into his lap to fall back to sleep.

"He's so sleepy he thinks you're me," Butcher said. He smiled and fingered his mustache. "That's kids for you. They don't even care."

Green put his hand in front of the boy's mouth and felt the kid's breath on his palm, cool and weak.

Outside, full-on night. But his time with Butcher had filled Green with an irresponsible energy, and he wasn't ready to go home yet, to shoulder the weight that waited for him there.

He drove to Quick Trip to buy cigarettes. Inside, a skinny girl stood in front of an open wall cooler, bills in her fist. She sucked a lollipop aggressively. He listened to it clack against her teeth.

"Bird or Train?" she asked, turning to him when she felt his eye. "Up to you, biggie: Bird or Train?"

He moved behind her and together they looked at the brown and green bottles. "Both," he said finally. "On me." He pulled a bottle of Thunderbird and a bottle of Night Train and handed them to her, then lifted a twelve of Budweiser for himself.

In the parking lot, the girl gave the bottles to another girl who held a raccoon on a leash. Taking it all in, Green was overcome with a sudden, fierce hope.

"Awful cold," he said to the girls, not going anywhere just yet.

"The cold keeps the bad people away," said the girl with the raccoon. She put the bottles in her backpack.

"You know of anywhere where there's not bad people?" drawled the girl with the lollipop in her mouth. *Clack, clack.* "Are you aware of anywhere like that?"

"I know some places," he said. The girls didn't have a car, so it was easy to get them into his. He drove them along the train tracks leading out of town to his one-room bank. He'd driven the same way a month earlier when he'd first spotted the OPEN HOUSE sign pasted to the bank's face. The building was low-slung and sided with weatherboard and had a round red-glass window in the front door. That day he'd stood at the window and watched the trains stop at the neighboring elevator to unload grain. He'd considered buying the building with Roy, but when he discovered the cut-rate price and the owners' desperation, he bought it alone. Across the tracks was a sod farm, and though it had already gone brown, he knew it would be different in the spring.

The girls arranged themselves on the air mattress in the vault while he lit the candle and plugged in a portable heater. He offered them blankets from a cache he kept in a garbage bag near the front door, then dragged a folding chair to the edge of the mattress. He set the case of beer on the seat and lowered himself to the floor.

"It's so nice being out of that boring town," the girl with the lollipop said, opening a bottle.

"Dead Moines," said her friend, hiking up her skirt and crossing her thin blue ankles. She pulled an apple from her pack and gave it to the raccoon, who seemed subdued. Green wondered if she had broken the animal's spirit or just fed him some kind of pill.

"It's such a wonder," the girl with the lollipop said. "Like here I am, holding this bottle right here in my hands, and then a second later it's inside me, making me all warm and wise and everything."

"That's a lie from hell," her friend said. "Alcohol has no effect on you."

"Don't you talk to me like that. Don't you look at me all

superior," the girl said. "Professional jealousy," she explained to Green. "From one fuck-up to another."

"OK," he said. "I get it." He reached for the bottle the girl was holding and took a long drink.

"Just wait until you kiss her," her friend said. "She's got a tongue exactly like leather."

"Will you shut up?" the girl said. "I like him." She turned to Green. "I like you. I do. I can see you know how to say farewell to all this. To everything. You'll be able to say goodbye when the time comes."

"Goodbye," he said.

"Oh, no, no," she said. "Time hasn't come yet." She stood and shrugged off her blanket, then turned away and lifted her shirt over her head. She bent to untie her boots. Her spine was a stack of dark nickels.

Still watching her, he reached above his head for a bottle of beer, but his fingers weren't working, and he knocked it to the floor. He tried to sweep the broken glass with his hands and immediately cut himself. He wrapped his hand in the tail of his shirt.

"Oh, no, no," the lollipop girl said. Her breasts shone. "You have to touch the injured part to the thing that injured it."

Her friend unbuttoned her own shirt and removed it. "That makes it heal."

The lollipop girl made him press a piece of bottle to the cut. Blood came over the glass, sweet and slow. Then the girl moved away from him and took hold of her friend. The girl began to hum. His eyes were wet.

"I feel like I'm always wrong," he said.

The girls moved together. Things were hazy, thick, but he

could sense some design in their motion, in their soft and synchronized breath. His hot face disturbed him. Looking away, he noticed the peculiar position of the raccoon on the floor, its limbs misaligned, it relative tension and slack incorrect.

"I believe the raccoon has died," he said.

The friend rose quickly from the lollipop girl and crawled across the air mattress to the animal. "Sometimes things that look dead are actually alive," she said, annoyed. She gave the raccoon a hard poke.

The raccoon convulsed, then somehow gathered itself, rose, and took a step before collapsing.

"See?" the friend said. "What did I say?"

Green decided he had to get home before morning. The girls said they'd sleep in the bank and hitchhike back to town with the dawn. He didn't care. He wrapped a blanket around his shoulders, climbed into his car, and turned the key. Driving, he suddenly realized how old he was getting, his night vision already on the wane. Traffic lights presented themselves blurrily, like flowers in a storm.

When he entered his house, they were all there, awake in his kitchen, sitting fast in their collective grimness: Roy and Molly and Nora. Always Nora.

"So what you been up to?" she said brightly. She crossed her arms on the kitchen table, then uncrossed them and put her chin in her hand.

"It's been a bad night," he said.

"For once he's telling the truth," she said. "And he doesn't even know it."

"It's been a bad night," he said again. He went to Nora,

actually knelt before her. "You know what I mean, don't you? Don't you?"

"He means he was out fucking," she explained to Roy and Molly, with a lovely, delicate sweep of her hand.

"I feel like I'm always wrong," he said to Nora.

"You stink like wine," Molly said, behind him, gently. "You have blood on your shirt."

"I always feel like I'm wrong," he repeated.

"You do seem to have an instinct for ruin," Nora said. She smiled benevolently. Then the smile was gone. "What are you here for? What do you intend to do?"

If he didn't move, she might see there was possibility in him. If he was quiet, she might hear him change.

"Green," Roy broke in, "our ship is sinking. While you were out doing nothing or everything, the Coronado burned. It's uninhabitable. Completely trashed."

It was like it had been written down somewhere. He'd spend his whole life in a basement, scratching letters onto fake gold.

"Did anyone die?" he thought to ask, dazed.

"People are fine. Building's shot," said Roy.

"It was really more smoke than flame," Molly said. "But it ended up bad."

It always seemed to, didn't it? He was still on his knees.

Roy drove. Green was in the back seat, next to Nora. She sat silent. He stared out the window. A car with no hood passed them by.

When they arrived at the Coronado, no one moved to exit the car except for him. "Aren't you all coming?" he asked.

"We've seen it already," Roy said, exasperated.

Nora said, "We were here while it went down."

He left the car and walked toward the apartment building. The air closed around him. Snow fell carelessly, without any real effort. The fire had left the complex featureless and turned its siding black. In front, tenants' burnt belongings were piled high under a blue tarp and gave off a wet, heavy odor like rich soil. He didn't know then that the odor would linger for weeks, even after Butcher killed himself, even after Roy and he dissolved the real estate partnership and split the insurance, even after he sold the one-room bank building to an independent travel agent at a loss.

He glanced back at the car. The dome light was on, and Nora leaned between the front seats. Roy stroked her hair. Twenty years ago, when Roy was first diagnosed with polio, he was put into quarantine. Their parents would take Green to the hospital where Roy was, and they would stand on the lawn and look up at Roy's window through binoculars. Eventually his parents were allowed to visit Roy in person, but it was too risky for Green. He stayed on the lawn. Through the binoculars he'd see his brother, ashy and thin at the lighted window, his parents behind him. They were as far away to Green as the moon.

The first thing Green noticed, pulling up to Butcher's place that weekend, was the absence of the garage. Where it used to stand, a slew of boards lay in disarray, as if they had washed up on land. When he rang the bell, one of the older children answered. He was saucer-eyed and skinny, with black hair that had been cut, Green could tell, by a man.

"Daddy's sleeping," the boy told him. Green stepped inside. He didn't know how it was possible, but the house was emptier and more cold. The rest of Butcher's kids were marching in front of a small fire in the living room fireplace, plastic bags stuffed into their shoes. The littlest girl had a bath towel wrapped around her head.

"Did the furnace break?" Green asked. "Where's your dad?"

"We don't have a furnace," the boy said.

"Of course you do," Green said, and headed for the boiler room. But the kid was right. Butcher had cut the pipes and hauled the furnace away.

"Dad sold it a while ago," the boy said, beside him. "We've been using fires to stay warm. We have to have a fire all the time."

"I don't believe it," Green said, pacing in the space where the furnace used to be.

"Look at the house!" the boy said, voice rising. "Dad ripped it all up and burned it! The walls, the stairs, the floors!"

"He was burning everything he took out?" Green stopped, in momentary admiration of Butcher's ingenuity and resolve. You have to admire the people that fool you, he knew, or you're even more foolish than you were before.

"Yesterday I helped him get down the garage," the boy said. "It should last for a time."

"I need to talk to your dad," Green said.

"I told you he was sleeping."

Green pushed past the boy. He found Butcher in what used to be the first floor bathroom. The double-swing door had been removed, and the toilet too. The towel racks had been unscrewed from the walls. In the space above the sink, where a mirror used to hang, was a perfect white circle. Butcher was zipped into a sleeping bag in the built-in tub. Green could see only a fistful of his hair.

"Wake up, Mat," he said. "Let's talk."

Butcher said nothing.

"I'm not playing now. This is too much." He knelt over the tub and moved the bag away from Butcher's face. Butcher was on his side, eyes half-open, teeth out in the air. Green touched his cool cheek with his thumb.

It was over. The house would never be repaired. Green saw the future: someday he'd die too. He covered Butcher's face and backed out of the room.

Butcher's kids stomped in front of the fire with the earnestness of a marching band. When Green lifted the littlest one into his arms, the rest fell in and followed him from the house to his car.

The streets were near-empty, and everything seemed whiter in the morning's cold, revelatory light. They drove over the Des Moines River to the city's east side.

Butcher's kids directed Green to their grandfather's apartment, where he set aside a room for his church. The apartment was over a sign-painting business the grandfather owned, and a wooden sign hung in the store's front window: CLOSED SUNDAYS IN HONOR OF OUR LORD.

The kids led him around the building to a fire escape. At the top was a small landing where an old man in a down jacket attended a Weber grill with a long-handled fork. The kids scrambled up the fire escape in front of Green, hugged the old man, then crawled through an open window. When he reached the top, Green could see a dozen people inside, milling around a big table laid with platters of deviled eggs and brownies and cubed cheese. Butcher's kids stood at the end of the table, mechanically eating potato chips out of a stainless steel bowl.

"I think something happened to your son," Green said.

Butcher's father stood easy, fork dangling at this side, an oven mitt on one hand.

"I'm sorry," said Green. "I wish I had different news."

The man smiled, faint and knowing. That smile on some people would have infuriated Green, but it looked right on Butcher's father, like he had earned it, like he had moved beyond this place to some easier world.

The old man opened the grill. The odor of sweet, wilting onions nearly brought Green to his knees. When you find a wise man, you should always ask a question. His poor teacher had instructed him thus. So he did.

"Maybe you know," Green said. "I don't get it. I feel like I'm always wrong. Is that how everybody feels?"

Butcher's father took a bottle of barbecue sauce from the window sill and held it to him. "My fingers," he said. "Could you?"

Green opened the bottle and gave it back.

THE FIFTH WALL

Sam's Tackle Box was wall-to-wall merchandise, packed so tight it fooled most customers into thinking that everything for sale was already on display. But Elana Hall wasn't fooled. Though the store stank of bait and brine, she could still catch the sour odor of methamphetamine, which Sam himself cooked regularly in a well-vented room above the sales floor.

Elana came to the Tackle Box with her daughter Jeanette every week, though neither had much affection for fish. Still, the kid went wild in the place, and broke away from her mother as soon as they passed through the door. Elana, troubled and aching, paused next to an arrangement of musky lures and watched her go. Weren't children's senses supposed to be more acute than adults'? Shouldn't Sam's reek and clutter be too much for her girl? A dim memory surfaced from her own past, a trip to New York City, to Chinatown, the smell of fish so overwhelming that she begged her dad to return to Des Moines straight away. The fact that her daughter could handle Sam's—the fact that she sometimes seemed to love it—suggested that Jeanette was already leaving childhood behind. Physical senses dulling, their loss soon to be offset by increased insight and guile. A pain pulsed behind Elana's eyes. It frightened her, this coming Jeanette. This clever spy replacing her dreamy little tot, who understood and wanted not much at all.

"Friends!" Sam's third wife called from behind the register. Her name was Janice and she wore studded wristbands, a leotard, and a long, low ponytail, as if at any minute she might either punch somebody or pull out a sticky mat and pop into downward-facing dog.

Elana allowed a thin smile of anticipation. Janice pushed a button beneath the counter, and they both listened to a faint bell ring overhead. There was the solid sound of boots hitting the floor. A door closing. The *ee-aw* of the stairs. Then Sam himself, from behind a green curtain on the side wall, still handsome and imposing at sixty. And Elana as happy to see him as a kid at the ceilidh, when he'd grab her to join a Gordon dance with his now-dead first wife and her dad.

She moved toward him quickly. But out from an aisle ran her daughter, crashing into his legs. Sam lifted Jeanette, and she opened up to flaunt her horrible new braces.

"Mom said they make me look beautiful!" she squealed.

"Your mom's a real sweet lady," Sam said smoothly. "Your mom's something else, that's for sure." He set the girl down. "In fact, I'd like to talk to your mom in private. I have an idea for your birthday present that I need to float."

"We got some Fuzz-E-Grubs in," Janice called enticingly. "I haven't put them out yet, but I'll let you take a look."

Her daughter rushed to the counter, and Elana followed Sam through an aisle of rigs and out a rear screen door to the Mirage. Thirty years ago he'd created it by fencing off half his parking lot and planting oak trees and grass. The last six months had seen the addition of motion-sensitive lights and barbed wire. The lights were designed to function only at night, but through the years, the oaks had grown aggressively, and the Mirage was overhung with a dense awning of leaves that nearly blocked the sun. As Elana and Sam entered, individual floods clicked on and spotlighted their movements—her sitting in a ratty mesh lounger, him hauling himself into the bass boat he'd parked on blocks.

This was in June, during a summer when the seventeen-year cicadas emerged from underground. The trees were filled with buzz, males drumming their abdomens while females laid eggs and died. But in spite of the noise, the headache Elana had been fronting all day stepped back. Around Sam, things settled into place. He took over whatever story you were telling so you could sit down and shut up.

She rolled her sleeve to her elbow. Sam unsnapped the boat's cover and climbed into the hold. A month ago she'd lost her job at Hy-Vee for spitting at a customer who complained about her bagging pace. Jeanette's braces came next. Still, even without cash, Sam kept advancing her. She knew he had a reason for stringing her along—the man was no saint—but she figured being aware of it meant that she was complicit. Being complicit in her own destruction made the danger seem less.

Sam climbed down from the boat with a syringe and a strip of tubing. When he offered them, she shook her head.

"Do you mind?" she asked. "My eyes are wrecked."

Obligingly, he bent to her, circling her bicep with tube. She bit one end and tasted rubber. Sam slapped the crook of her arm, until he stopped.

First came the Nip. Then the Whirl. Elana pumped her fists and rose from the chair, head bobbing, until she bumped a low branch and loosed a rain of cicada shells. Sighing, Sam plucked the molted skins from her hair.

"Seventeen years ago," he said, pinching a dry skin to dust. "Where was Elana then?"

Her head rang as images flashed from that summer. Third place in Jig at a dancing comp in Chicago. Pink champagne from the gas station, drunk in Greenwood Park. The driver's ed teacher, Mr. Hunt, yelling about her lead foot and rolling stops.

"That was not a full stop!" she croaked now, remembering his hoarse voice from the passenger seat. "In California, maybe that half-assed stop would fly. But not here, I assure you, not here!"

Sam cast a sharp eye upon her. "Funny you mention California," he said. "You ever been?"

"Un uh. Un uh." She stepped away from him, to give everything its space.

Sam carefully retucked his shirt before lowering himself into a chair. "Let me be straight," he said. "I'm not one for cutting off people. But I can't see as to how you're going to pay this large debt you've acquired."

So this was the day! A flicker of fear, but the speed transformed it to energy. "Maybe we can brainstorm," she chirped.

"I'll start." Sam stroked his beard, the pale gray of it strange against his hard tanned face. "Let me paint the big picture. Demand is high, which is good, but the bad news is I can't keep up on my own. Most operations around here are sourced in southern Cal. It's time for me to plug into that game. The catch is that particular pipeline's no secret to anyone, narcs included, and they've got highways between here and LA all staked out. Some unfortunates try the bus as safe passage. Remember the guy nabbed on Greyhound with ten pounds of crank in his socks?"

"What about flying?"

"X-rays, dogs. No, the road is the only way to go. The one question: what's the best cover?"

He went on to describe his strategy of outfitting a vehicle and its passengers as if the whole enterprise were an innocent family trip. Plenty of luggage in the trunk, plenty of snacks in a cooler, guidebooks and maps prominently displayed. The problem was, he said, that even if he and Janice tricked themselves out as tourists, the disparity in their ages made them appear suspect. It wasn't Janice, he continued, but himself. There was a criminal air about him he'd never been able to shake. That, along with a tendency to get shifty-eyed in authority's presence, meant he'd be forced to sit this trip out.

Elana tried to stay with the speech, but the meth jumped her ahead to his as-yet unspoken proposal that she go to California in his place. The idea both terrified and attracted her. That's how it was with most things those days.

"I want to give you the chance to clear your debt," Sam said, leaning forward to set his elbows on his knees. "I'll forgive everything if Jeanette rides to California with Janice."

"No," she said automatically.

"Imagine. A cop pulls them over. What's this? A mother and daughter taking a summer trip. What could be nicer? More straight up?"

"A good mother wouldn't risk her kid that way." But already she perceived a slight inner crumbling. "How could I be a good mother and let her go?"

"A good mother wants what's best for her child. Think. What do you want for Jeanette?"

She envisioned an island with coconuts and wild horses.

"For her to end up someplace else."

"Right," said Sam. "Someplace else entirely. This trip could show her a lot of different ways to live." He reclined in the chair. "Besides, you know I loved your father. I'd never do anything to hurt his own grandkid."

"What about me?" she heard herself whine. "I'm his only daughter. Look what you've done to me."

Sam stood and took hold of her wrist. At first she thought he was comforting her, but as his grip tightened, she received the real message: Pain.

"You dug your own hole," he said evenly. "I brought the shovel, but you put it to dirt."

"Without the shovel I couldn't have gone very deep," she pointed out.

"Don't be stupid."

"I'm not stupid," she mumbled. "I'm weak." Then some sort of aural hallucination overtook her, reducing their discussion to one word—California!—cried with delight. *California! California! California!* With each repetition the word sounded less strange and the voice more familiar, until she recognized it as her daughter's, from inside the store. Was it possible her daughter had stumbled into her consciousness, discovering a decision she thought she hadn't yet made?

"I'm going to California!" Jeanette cried. Elana wrenched away from Sam and peered through the screen. Her daughter ran toward her, braids flying, so quickly there was no time for warning.

Jeanette crashed into the door at full speed. Dazed, she tried to pull away, but her braces were tangled in the screen.

"Oh dear," Janice said, behind her. "I'll get pliers."

Jeanette screamed. The sound pierced Elana, but before she could move, Sam was kneeling before the door.

"Honey," he said urgently, "calm down, or you'll get hurt worse. How about I give you the rest of your birthday present? Then play you a little something on my pipes?"

Jeanette's next sob stopped in her throat. "Okay," she said, sniffling.

Sam ambled toward his boat, the motion lights flashing like he was a paparazzo's prey. After a moment, Elana willed herself toward her daughter. Jeanette's lips were stretched back from her mouth. Her gums and teeth were flat against the wire, like a caged monkey's in a lab.

"Sweetpea," Elana told her, "I'm going to open the door really slowly. You walk forward when I do." When she turned the handle and pulled, Jeanette inched over the threshold into the Mirage. Elana held her hand and squatted opposite the screen.

"Your hand thwet," her daughter said in an accusing tone, tongue thrusting against the screen.

"I'm sweating," Elana said quickly. "You scared the crap out of me with that wail." She let go to wipe her palm on her jeans, then clutched Jeanette's hand again. "Why do you say you're going to California?"

"Janith thaid you thaid OK. For my birthday."

"That really sounds fun?"

"Your faith ith weird."

"You ought to see yours," Elana said. She licked her lips. "So you want to go? You wouldn't miss not having me along?"

Before her daughter could answer, Sam returned, a purple plastic suitcase in hand. When he unzipped the case, it was stuffed with new clothes. He removed a pair of red canvas platform sneakers for Jeanette's approval. They were far too high for an eight-year-old girl.

"I love them!" her daughter exclaimed.

"Let me see those," said Elana.

"Careful," Sam said, handing her a sneaker. It was surprisingly light, and when she examined the sole, she saw it had been cut out and reglued. If she had a knife, she could wedge the tip in and peel back the rubber, but even without a knife she knew what was inside. A hollowed-out platform. An empty space. They were going to stash drugs in her daughter's shoes. It was wicked enough to make her woozy. Though if cops found drugs on Jeanette—she caught herself reasoning—they'd know her daughter was an unwitting pawn. The nearest adult would be the one accountable. And Elana would be miles away. If the cops came after her next, she could explain an old family friend had offered the trip as a gift. How could she be expected to know the journey's true aim?

She wanted to ask Jeanette leading questions, but her daughter was transfixed by the sight of Sam. Whistling, he sat in the lounger and assembled his bagpipes, fitting the melody pipe and drones to their stocks. Jeanette watched him fixedly, until Janice returned with the pliers and a small pair of wire snips.

Catching sight of the tools, Jeanette stiffened. "Nooo," she moaned.

"It's all right," Janice said. "I'm just going to untwist the wire and maybe cut away a bit of screen."

"Mom," Jeanette whispered.

"We need to get you out," Elana reassured her, squeezing her hand. "Would you feel better if I do it?"

Her daughter gave her a wary look. "What about Tham?"

He halted his assembling. "My fingers are too big, honey," he said. "I can't get in there."

"Do you want me to do it?" Elana asked again.

Something bleak descended onto her daughter, darkening her thin face.

"No," she said at last. "Janith can."

The other woman nudged Elana from her spot. When the pliers opened, Elana looked away. She shifted her attention to the lounger, where Sam was tuning his pipes. First a note on the chanter. Followed by a note from the tenor drone, not quite there. He adjusted the sliding joints and again played the chanter. Then another near miss. More adjustments, and the drone became shorter. Once more, the original note. The tenor note, played in response, remained a hair's-breadth off-key.

Elana's shirt was soaked in sweat. "Isn't it close enough?" she asked angrily.

Without responding, Sam mouthed the blowpipe and started "Scotland the Brave." The low notes thrummed in her chest the way they had in her childhood, when during the summer Sam and her dad practiced in the yard. She'd listened from the attic where she slept. All the heat in the house rose there, and she removed her nightgown and threw the sheets on the floor to get cool. She closed her eyes and held herself rigid in order to catch the tiniest draft if it passed. Most nights she'd be awake for hours. The heat rarely broke before dawn.

Now here was the same tune, the same player. She tried to bring back the sensation of being still. But the secret was gone.

"Finished," Janice announced, shaking out her wrist.

Jeanette didn't respond. She stared at Sam, who puffed his cheeks and pressured the bag beneath his arm. Noticing this, Elana slipped behind her daughter and eased her away from the door. Then she bent to her ear.

"You know, baby, they call California the Golden State, because they discovered gold there, yes, and because of all the yellow sand too, of course, but golden also because everybody wants to go there, to *be* there, and myself, I never have, so I think you're really very lucky, you're luckier than me, and—"

"Quit talking," Jeanette snapped. "I want to hear."

An hour later, Elana walked Grand Avenue alone. Out of a passing car, a driver tossed a lit cigarette. Elana pinched it from the sidewalk, hand trembling as she brought it to her lips. She nursed the stub for five blocks before throwing it away.

Once home, she tore open an envelope of lime Jell-O. She wet her finger and poked inside, licking off whatever stuck. After the dark streets, the kitchen seemed snug and intimate. Blue bowls dried in a wooden drainer, an herb garden grew in Styrofoam cups on the sill. Elana switched on the television. Let the thing glow and roar for a while.

She poured the rest of the Jell-O into a teacup. Onscreen,

an interior designer instructed his viewers not to forget the ceiling in their decorating plans. "Very important," the man declared. "*The ceiling is your fifth wall.*" The show cut to footage of a sloppy angel-themed mural, but Elana couldn't get past the words. If the ceiling was truly the fifth wall, then the floor, Lord help her, must be the sixth. At the thought, all six walls began moving closer. She fled, with her teacup, to the yard.

There, the cicadas' singing had taken on a rowdy, boastful aspect. Elana paced the perimeter of her bricked-up patio. Her daughter was staying with Sam and Janice and would leave at sunrise. They were aiming for North Platte by noon.

She'd done a terrible, evil thing. But suddenly, under the black sky, she felt blessed. Her debt was paid. More important, she'd finally hit rock bottom. After this, she and Jeanette could begin again. No more drugs. No Tackle Box. No Sam. She breathed, imagining clarity as a glittering steam free for her to inhale.

Back in the kitchen, she turned off the television and went to survey her daughter's room. Her sweet love! Hot tears spilled to her cheeks, and she staggered onto her daughter's bed. The body was exhausted, but the mind galloped. Even with closed eyes, she could see Jeanette's monkey face. Despairing, she looked to the ceiling for solace. In one corner hung a thread of lint, twitching in a feeble breeze.

Jeanette's riding shotgun, next to Janice, and her mouth hurts. In her pocket there's wax to protect her cheeks from braces, but wax is nothing, it's really a joke. Her mother said to try aspirin, but Jeanette doesn't ever take it, and she doesn't ask Janice for anything now. The truth is she thinks this must be what it feels like to be older. The ache makes her feel tired and wise.

Janice says, "Out here, in spring, people set fires to their lawns. Burn off winter weeds so grass comes back green and strong."

Jeanette thinks Janice is sort of ugly, with those droopy eyes and her bad skin.

"Sometimes on windy days," Janice says, "the fires get big and take houses."

Jeanette ignores her, looking up at a barn as red as soup, with wooden slats that let sunlight through.

Just over the hill, Janice slams the brakes hard. Tea splashes from the mug she's holding onto her sweater and the legs of Jeanette's jeans.

"Look," she says.

Jeanette does. The sky's purple with sunrise. Thick haze drifts over the road.

"Unless you want to go crazy," Janice says, "make sure you're often in the presence of beauty."

Jeanette nods.

"Or in the presence of ugliness," Janice continues, "if it is the truth."

Jeanette shivers because her mind's been read. She says, "I think you're ugly sometimes."

"I'm true. And truthfully, sometimes you're ugly too."

"But I'm not true," Jeanette says.

Janice sips tea. "Dishonesty has its own kind of beauty," she says. "Especially if it reveals a deeper truth."

"Can we have tacos for lunch?" Jeanette asks her.

"What?"

"Can we have tacos?"

"Why do I bother?" Janice sighs, but with affection in her

voice, maybe. She pulls Jeanette close and twists a piece of her hair to its root.

Like she had been attacked by a drunken boxer, Elana hurt. Fever burned in her eyeballs and the membranes of her nose. Lying in her daughter's bed, she chewed on a piece of lip until it ripped free. The new morning filtered in, bringing no hope whatsoever. When she pressed a thumb to her lip, it came back with blood. The promises she'd made to herself? Ha. Overnight, the blessing she had received was withdrawn.

Sam lived in one half of a duplex a few blocks from the store. Elana hesitated on his porch before ringing the bell. He'd instructed her to lie low until Janice and Jeanette returned. He planned to close the Tackle Box and spend the weekend piping at the Highland Games. Nobody was supposed to contact anybody. There would be no postcards or calls from the road.

When the door opened, Sam was already wearing his kilt. He looked angry, but unsurprised.

"What are you doing here?" he said. "We had a deal."

"I don't want her to go," Elana said.

"You know they already left. Why did you come?"

She opened her mouth to answer, but lacked the energy to speak.

"Say, 'I'm powerless to face real life.' Say, 'I've sold my soul.'"

There was no call for him to talk like that. Her indignation gave her a moment's strength. "I don't feel powerless," she said slowly. "Not at all. Desperate, maybe. Like I could do anything. Even call the police."

Sam glared at her. "You'll get busted and lose her forever."

"In this life," she said, "all of us have things to lose."

"You dead-eyed . . ." For an instant, she thought he'd hit her, but somehow he regained control. "What I am doing?" he said, straining for an affable tone. "You and me, we're friends. For a long time now. We should help each other through this rough patch."

"I could use some help," she said.

"There's no reason to go through this alone. It will be a hard week for both of us." He smiled tensely. "How about this? Why don't you come with me to the Games? Might be a nice diversion for you."

So he understood it was safer to have her near. To keep her addled and quiet. Good.

Once she was inside, Sam said offhandedly, "Check out the third drawer in the john." There she found a glassine envelope and a kit. The tubing in her mouth tasted like a pacifier. Two fingers rapped against her skin sounded like trying to shake ketchup out. After she fixed, the exhilaration of the previous night made a more muted return. It was as if she squinted, she could see an endpoint to everything looming in the distance like some far-flung sign. One last week, she vowed. One last week, and she was through.

On the way to the Games, she jabbered to Sam about her redecorating plans for Jeanette's room, the wonders she'd work on that fucked ceiling—wait—*fifth wall.* He listened in silence.

"Here," he said finally, when they'd pulled into the fairgrounds' dusty parking field. He gave her a small baggie of pills. "In case you want to bring it down."

The entrance to the Games was flagged by banners announcing the weekend's reuniting clans. Sam paid her admission, and they entered the gauntlet of exhibitors and vendors peddling everything from bangers to medieval swords. In one spacious booth, a falconer in black gloves attended a hawk tied with bungee cord to a steel V-framed perch. As Elana approached, she saw the man fasten a silver bell to the hawk's leg. Above the bell, the bird's plumage was cream and brown, its posture freakily erect. Elana stepped closer. The hawk appeared sleek-bodied and hungry. He was a fearsome creature, even tied.

The falconer glanced at her. Then at Sam.

"What do you throw a drowning bagpipe player?" he asked.

Sam sighed before answering. "His bagpipes."

"You got it," the falconer said, standing tall. "Cheers. You know, they say the Scots have a good sense of humor because it's free." He reached behind him for a whiskey-filled qualich, but Sam declined his offer and took Elana's arm.

"Go ahead," she said. "I think I'll hang out here for a while."

"Let's go." He increased the strength of his hold.

"Ow," Elana said, loudly.

The falconer's eyebrows lifted. Across the row, a pretzel vendor paused as she counted a man's change. Sam assessed the scene. After a moment, he released Elana and brushed some dust from his shirt front. "Be at the stage in half an hour," he said through his teeth.

"Don't worry, pops," the falconer cracked. "I'll keep an eye on her." Beside him, the hawk lifted both wings until they nearly met overhead. Sam gave man and bird a measured gaze before finally walking away.

The falconer laughed. "Is your daddy piping today?"

"He's not my daddy," Elana said. "But he's piping for highland dancing." She accepted the qualich and drank. "You may not believe it, but I used to dance myself. Many years ago."

"I bet you were something in your hornpipe suit." The falconer was too young for her, but he had a sly manner than made her feel indulgent of his youth.

"What about you?" she asked, returning the cup. "You hunt or you only do the Games?"

"We fly most days. Even if it's just driving around the neighborhood with my arm stuck out, hunting sparrows from the glove."

She stared wide-eyed at the hawk. "You fly this thing at sparrows?"

"Other days we go to the country with a couple ferrets. Loose the ferrets to flush the jacks out of their holes. Then this beauty wastes them." He clapped his hands. "Rabbit stew all around."

"Wouldn't it be easier to use a gun?"

"Always easier to use a gun. But I'm not about easy." He shook his head, grinning. "No, I take my pleasure in the process." He bent toward her. "And, if I may ask, what do you take your pleasure in?"

She shrugged. "I'd say product. Mostly."

"That was my guess," he said. "But maybe I can change your mind." He assumed a wide stance and cleared his throat. "There's this process called manning. It's when you train the raptor to tolerate your presence. Convincing her it's in her best interest to stick around."

She was interested.

"Like you might bind her wings in a sock so she can't fly off at the sight of you."

"I'm not going anywhere," Elana said.

The falconer seemed amused. "Then on to the unconventional ways." He lowered his voice. "I know one way to cut the manning time in half. Learned it from a fellow over in Cairo. Seeling, he called it."

"I'm listening," she whispered back.

The falconer placed a glove over her face. It was large enough to cover all her features. She let her tongue flick out to taste the grain.

"In seeling," he said, "you sew a raptor's eyes shut with a single piece of thread."

Elana punched away the glove. "What the hell?"

The falconer blinked. "Don't get the wrong idea." He gestured to the hawk, who observed him blankly. "There's no master-slave thing happening here."

"I hope that bird claws out your eyeballs!" Elana cried.

"You got the wrong idea," the falconer insisted. "I live my whole life around hers."

Elana swiveled wildly. People were gathering, and in the distance, she saw a man with a red SECURITY sash take note. Meanwhile, the falconer pleaded for understanding. The hawk stretched, extending its tail feathers in a fan. Elana broke into a panicky jog that carried her past the heavy athletics field, the exhibition hall, and a Campbell clan reunion before she arrived, sweating, at the outdoor dancing stage. The competition hadn't started, but the stage was crowded with girls practicing jumps and high steps. The girls wore gray sweatpants under their kilts, and their hair was twisted into what looked like painful buns.

She made her way to a patch of lawn near the front of the amphitheater. Beside her, a couple on a blanket fed each other fresh shortbread and shared a cup of lemon tea. Elana's pulse felt erratic, and her forearms itched. She choked down two

Valium, but forbade herself from scratching. It was small punishment for her flirting. For flirting while her child might be in danger. She wept softly at the idea.

"Your daughter up there?" the male half of the couple asked, mistaking her tears for pride.

"Where?" she said eagerly, before catching herself. "I mean, no, I don't have kids." Mentioning Jeanette would only lead to further questions. How old? What's she like? Where is she now?

"Sorry," the man said. "None of my business."

"Nope, no kids," she repeated. "Maybe someday."

Over the loudspeaker, the MC called for the Novices to gather. He introduced three judges, who assumed center seats. Finally he brought on Sam, who appeared with a wink and his bagpipes, hitting his spot at the rear of the stage.

The first group competed in the Fling. Elana tried to lose herself in the kids' goofy missteps, but without luck. Denying her daughter's existence had left her sick. Why didn't she mention Jeanette and, if the man asked more, explain that she was at camp? She considered leaning over now and telling him, but he would think she was crazy.

Onstage, Sam ended the tune with a flurry of grace notes. He counted *one-two-three,* and the little girls bowed. Next, a cluster of Intermediates mounted the stage, one of whom looked so much like Jeanette—the braids, the braces, the hyper air—that Elana had to lower her eyes. The action was enough to ease her into sleep.

Mid-Nebraska, there's a red school bus parked way off the road, and that's where they pause for a while. Janice's girlfriend lives there. She and Janice sprawl on beanbags and smoke clove cigarettes, listening to Joni Mitchell's *Blue.*

"Come here," Janice says.

Jeanette sits beside her, and Janice twists her into a yoga position, feet behind her head. Jeanette's back against the wall keeps her upright. Her tailbone's rock hard on the floor.

"Can you imagine?" the girlfriend says. "I mean, really."

"Great popularity in her future," Janice says.

"Yeah?" Jeanette wonders.

"No," Janice says. "Your fate is to be alone."

"Hey," the girlfriend says, pissed, "don't saddle the poor kid with that."

"I'm liberating her," says Janice. "Being alone you're free to take risks. That's the kind of people the world needs."

"Not nice," the girlfriend says, rising from the beans. "Not nice at all!" She adjusts her vest and wobbles out of the bus.

"Women," Janice sighs. Then she crawls toward the door, calling, "Kelly? Honey?"

Jeanette watches her go, not worrying, because she knows she'll return. But soon she hears glass break, a door slam, a car starting and driving away.

The problem: she has flexibility, but not strength. Her arms are trapped by her thighs, and she doesn't have enough muscle to lift her feet over her head. "Lift," she mutters, "lift!" Nothing. Joni sings about kissing some pig on some street.

A few minutes later an older girl saunters in, buttoning a plaid cover onto a Bermuda bag. She stops and studies the scene before setting down her purse and grabbing Jeanette's shoes. Her freed feet *thunk-thunk* on the floor.

"Thanks," Jeanette says, toes stinging. She tries to stand, but the girl says no.

"Always end with the corpse pose," the girl says. She tells Jeanette to lie on her back, arms out to the side. "Make your legs heavy," she says. "Open your shoulders. Now relax and let your tongue settle down."

Elana started awake. Onstage the Premier class had finished Flora's Fancy and held their skirts out stiffly, like clean white tents. Sam whispered *one-two-three* from his corner. The girls performed lovely bows. It was the final dance of the morning, and Sam lumbered off the stage.

Red-faced from anger and lack of breath, he came to where Elana was sitting. "Nodding off up here in front of everyone," he chastised her.

"I can't do this," she said. "We have to stop it. Something terrible's going to happen on this trip."

"Come on," Sam said, yanking her to her feet. "There's another piper for the afternoon session. I'm off until tomorrow. Let's split."

On the way to the car, they passed the falconer. Elana ducked her head and tried to hurry by.

"Hey, pops," the falconer called. "What do you have when a piper is buried to his neck in sand?"

Sam pivoted toward him. The falconer's hopeful smile began to fade. It took Sam three steps to cover the distance between them. Then, with a neat jab, he slammed the hawk. The bird's feet stuttered before it dropped like a rock from the perch, swinging upside-down from its cord.

"Not enough sand," said Sam. He kept his fist clenched, like the falconer was next. But the anguished man was cradling the hawk, trying to revive it, and eventually Sam's fingers relaxed.

Back in the car, Elana tried to organize her thinking, but the wind speeding through the windows left her thoughts in disarray. She couldn't pin down her fear. It was a subtle, sneaky dread.

"I want out of this," she finally said. "Why are you getting me deeper in?"

"You want out?" Sam shouted suddenly, slapping the wheel. "Bullshit. You're working this situation for all it's worth. Threatening to spill the beans, faking second guesses. Anything so I'll keep you tweaking until that poor girl gets back."

"For one week, Sam. One last week. When she gets back, it's over."

His eyes rolled. "Honey, deep down you think you've hit the jackpot. You think you've discovered the way to get your shit for free." He sounded an ugly snort. "The last week? It's the first of many weeks. Check yourself. You'll see."

She did, imagining her daughter's return. The car pulling up, her daughter bursting from the side door, sunglasses atop her head like a crown. Her daughter ran to her. She hugged Jeanette, then held her at arm's length to soak her in. Then, as she saw herself in this vision, she knelt eagerly to untie her daughter's platform shoes.

Elana vomited onto the floor mat. What emerged was watery and green.

The drive continued, but Sam took a hand from the wheel

to rub her back as she heaved. "Calm yourself," he crooned, "everything's fine." His voice like a lullaby. "You know, your dad and I had some talks before he passed. He was worried. Your trouble had been going on for so long. He knew you'd never quit. He knew I was getting into the business. We both knew you'd find your demons somewhere."

A dark spot appeared. "Don't you say it," she warned. "Even if it's true."

"In the end we figured: why not Sam? If I was the one, at least I could manage your intake. Adjust the potency, if need be."

"You think I believe," she choked, "that my dad asked you to string me out?"

"He trusted me," Sam went on. "He knew I'd been looking out for you all your life. Just today, in fact, I was remembering when I used to play your dancing comps. You never caught on, but I'd always play a bit faster for your group. Get you jumping higher. Get the blood to your cheeks."

The car stopped, and when she lifted her head, she saw they'd arrived at the Tackle Box. When she faced Sam, his expression was fond.

"I'll always protect you, Elana. And if I'm still around when you're gone, I'll protect your daughter too."

Her throat burned. "When I'm gone?"

"You've picked a dangerous life." He gazed at her ruefully.

"You plan on killing me, Sam?"

He chuckled. "I don't think my involvement will be required."

"Go ahead," she challenged him. "Sew my eyes shut while you're at it. Sew them shut so I can't see your broke-down lying face."

"There's a face you don't want to see," he agreed. "But we both know that face isn't mine."

He helped her from the car to the Tackle Box entrance, where he ushered her in, flipping on one weak light. Dumbly, Elana followed him through the dim aisles and out to the Mirage. Sam steered her to a lounger and offered a beer.

"Upstairs if you need me," he said then, heading back into the store. "Duty, it always seems to call."

The beer rested cold in her lap, and soon she was plagued by chills. In the trees, the cicadas droned loudly. She struggled out of the lounger and into the Tackle Box. Disoriented by the lack of light, she made her slow way to the store's telephone. She stared at it for a while before lifting the receiver. Nothing. When she examined the base, she saw the cord to the wall jack was gone.

There was footfall on the stairs. A moment later, Sam stepped from behind his green curtain and saw the dead phone in her hand.

"Oh, honey," he said, smiling faintly. "Why do you try?"

The pope is coming to Denver tomorrow for a conference of Catholic youth. Janice pleads with front desks from North Platte to Loveland, but the motels are packed with clean teens. "Fine," Janice declares, "we'll keep driving. All the way to California if need be!"

By Utah, she's exhausted. The road's straight, so she decides to let Jeanette take the wheel. Jeanette sits on top of her new purple suitcase, with Janice shotgun, her foot on the pedal until she sets cruise control. Then it's Jeanette alone. The thrill reminds Jeanette of mornings when her mom is sleeping, when the whole house is hers. She drinks coffee and gets the paper and cuts the herb garden. After a while she wakes her mom with a cup of spearmint brew.

When Jeanette sees a roadside phone, she turns off cruise and slides from the suitcase until her shoe hits the brake.

"I want to call home," she announces.

"No time," says Janice. "No money. No need." She reaches over and lightly beats Jeanette's leg. "Let's go."

"I'm not a drum."

"My sweet bongo," Janice sings. "My little snare." She returns Jeanette to her perch, presses the pedal, and turns the car back to the road.

After cruise control's set, Jeanette shuts her eyes for one second. Two seconds. Three. The dark part's not that bad. She's only scared when her eyes open again.

When she spots a shooting star, she pokes Janice. "Did you see?"

Janice squints at the windshield. "Make a wish," she says.

Jeanette watches another star drop. And another. Then she thinks she's crazy because there are dozens, there are hundreds, exploding like bulbs. When one falls onto the hood, she slides for the brake.

Then she's standing on the hot road. From there, she can see the stars are fireflies. Swarms of fireflies. She catches one. Through her fingers comes bleary light.

Janice gets out and stands beside her, and Jeanette tells her how once her mom killed some fireflies and smeared them on Jeanette's cheeks.

"Your mother," Janice frowns.

"Don't move," her mom had told her. Then she had run inside.

She came back with the medicine cabinet's ripped-off mirror. She held it up to Jeanette so she could see her own face glow.

First the sky was a ceiling of black vinyl. Then it became the sky she remembered—endless blue.

"Welcome back," a voice said.

Elana rose from a pillow of wadded rags. Sam was at the other end of the boat, rolling up the cover. At the sight of him, she vaguely recalled a speed-fueled Tea Party, with her climbing into the bass boat and chucking paraphernalia onto the grass. Then Sam wrestling her to the deck. Pushing pills past her stiff lips. Black vinyl snapped tight above. And finally sleep, a long one, utterly free of dreams.

"Quite a night," said Sam. For once, he looked his age.

"I thought I was dead," she said. "The pills, I mean."

He crossed the deck to enfold her in what felt like a poor replica of a hug.

"Such paranoia," he said. "Not necessary. The goal is to get through this with no drama, no fuss. You think I want a body on my hands? And an orphan? The whole deal would blow apart." He embraced her more tightly, his beard roughing her skin. "Yeah, yesterday I was trying to make you a little scared. To get you behaving. But the truth is I need you alive." He stepped back and rubbed his hands briskly. "Now quit worrying. You need a morning shot?"

She said no. Whatever he'd given her was still in her blood. She pushed past him into the Tackle Box and found the bathroom, where she massaged her gums with toothpaste and sprayed Janice's perfume. She was dirty, but she vowed not to take a bath until her daughter returned.

The drive to the Highland Games was a silent one, and the silence continued as they walked through the fairgrounds. Elana noticed the falconer's absence from his former post and found herself wishing him good health.

They were late, but there was a seat in the front row. Sam left her there and hurried to fix his bagpipes and take the stage. The Lilt was the first number, danced by the Intermediates, and as they lined up, Elana spotted the girl who resembled Jeanette a second time. The girl could pass for Jeanette's sister, in fact, and seeing her, Elana wished she were. It wasn't fair to have only one child. Alone, with no siblings to comfort her or boost her anger, the only child was compelled to forgive.

When the dance ended, the couple beside her stood and moved back several rows. Elana wondered if she stank, if the perfume was too much. But then another family hurried to the rear, and following their nervous glances, she saw a good-sized swarm of yellow jackets overhead.

"They'll only sting you once," the MC chortled, noticing the minor exodus. "Pay no mind." A group of Premiers took the stage for the Irish Jig.

Elana studied the swarm above her. It was flattening like a chunk of butter heated in a pan. The yellow jackets looped in larger, lower circles until they were streaming over the theater's front half. A few landed on her arm, but she didn't flick them, unlike most of the audience, who dashed, swatting madly, to the back.

There was a brief conference at the MC's table with the judges and Sam. Then the MC returned to his microphone. "We're going to keep going," he announced. "The girls are OK up here. Those little suckers are avoiding the stage." He paused.

"Plenty of seats in the back, though, if anyone would be more comfortable there."

She stayed where she was. The Jig was her favorite dance. Sam launched into it, and the dancers shook their fists and stomped their feet, a burlesque of angry workers crushing snakes. All smiled broadly, except for a single girl whose grim expression truly matched the dance's intent.

A cluster of yellow jackets settled at the base of Elana's neck, tickling beneath her chin. Another grouped loosely near her wrist. She didn't flinch. In her mind, she was mapping Sam's speed against a steady rhythm. At last she could hear it—he was rushing the Jig! Her mouth fell open when suddenly he pushed the tempo faster. Yet the grim girl met him, sweat beading on her muscled calves.

Then all at once, Sam slipped the blowpipe from his lips. The Jig trailed off with a tired squawk. Most of the dancers halted immediately, except for the grim girl, who performed a few steps without a tune. But then she paused too, and looked where everyone was looking. At Elana. Like she was onstage.

Such anxious faces! She wanted to tell them not to worry, but feared disturbing the things on her tongue.

"Easy now," Sam called. His voice quivered like an old man's.

It was amazing, all these creatures moving through her, even as she remained still.

THINK STRAIGHT

One of the architects did churches and churches only, a haggard man named Theo Carney whose table sat in the southern corner of the office to take advantage of a large Diocletian window and the sun's flat white light. Carney had a talent for designing spaces intimate enough to provide comfort, but with high ceilings that gave glory room to rise. The paradoxical nature of his work took a toll. In the mornings, the firm's partners and interns watched Carney drift to his table, pale and shaky, where he swallowed a series of round blue pills with his coffee, black. A half hour later, sparking with a new fire, Carney would bend to his desk and work feverishly until noon. Until noon, when the intern to whom the thankless task had fallen attempted to take his order for lunch.

"Mr. Carney," the intern would say, quietly at first. When

Theo didn't respond, one partner or another would look up from his table and smile, and the intern, noting it, realized it was all right to press on. "Mr. Carney," he repeated, louder. Carney remained motionless, except for his frenetic sketching hand. The intern might tap Theo's shoulder then and—upon receiving no response—get bolder, using a nearby dusting brush to poke his arm or winging an erasing shield into his lap. Finally, Carney still oblivious, a damp laughter building in the office, the intern would position himself in front of the window and hop, arms waving, casting long shadows across Carney's plans. Only then would Theo blink, puzzled, and say in his croupy voice, "Corned beef, please."

Green, one of the interns, observed the daily exercise from his own table and disapproved. Theo ordered the same meat every time, so what was the point, really, except to ease the rest of the office into the lesser seriousness of the lunch hour and somehow boost intern morale? Green's brother had been diagnosed with polio three weeks earlier, and Green's proximity to the tragedy, he believed, endowed him with more sensitivity than most sixteen-year-old boys. Also, in his view, architects were true artists, and artists' kinks should be celebrated, copied even, not lampooned. So when it was finally his turn to do lunches, he didn't run Theo through the drill. He gathered orders from the rest of the firm and walked to Andy's Eats to collect the food. After distributing most of it, he approached Carney's desk and knelt to leave a wrapped corned beef sandwich beside the man's shoes.

Catching a scent, Theo looked down. When he saw the sandwich, his clouded eyes cleared to reveal both his knowledge of and gratitude for being spared. It embarrassed Green. He turned to leave.

"Wait." Carney's voice was breathy. He studied Green for a moment, then focused on the floor plan stretched across his board: a top view of a one-story church.

"I need a perspective of this," Carney said. "Can you do it?"

Could he? Could he? Green had taken mechanical drawing the previous year in high school and, as a final project, drew floor plans and elevations and perspectives for a remodeling of his parents' garage into a bathhouse complete with indoor pool. His teacher praised his ambition, his parents ridiculed it, but they had allowed him to work the summer at the firm as a learning experience, though he wasn't learning much of anything at all. Most mornings he ran off blueprints on the blueprint machine. Afternoons, he delivered bid packages to the Master Builders of Iowa downtown.

"I suppose I could," said Green. He had learned one thing that summer from the other interns, two college boys who smoked Chesterfields and on dates took twin high school girls bowling—an ugly, transparent nonchalance.

Carney stared at him.

"I mean, sure I can," said Green. "I know how to. Terrific, yes."

"You know how to draw lines?"

"Definitely. All sorts."

"And do you know why you draw lines?" Carney asked.

"Well," Green answered cautiously, not wanting to betray his growing unease. "In this case it's for a perspective. To be able to show the client what is in your mind's eye."

Carney leaned toward him. "And how do you read my mind?"

That one was a doozy. When Green didn't answer, Carney beckoned him close.

"It's very easy," he said, fingering the floor plan. "You look here. Everything is here."

"Oh, of course," Green said quickly. "That will help."

Carney's expression changed, losing the warm aspect it had, for a moment, held. He rolled up the sketch. "Elevations are in the files," he said. "I'll need it by Friday."

Green accepted the drawing, trying to keep the joy from his face. He left the plan on his own table, then carried his sandwich to the back stoop. The concrete steps were hot in the August sun, and the light was so bright he kept his eyes half-closed. The other interns might enjoy lunch in comfort at their drafting table, but not Green, not even when he had no project laid there. Every object had a function, he believed, and not respecting that function undermined self-discipline. After that came confusion. After that, mistakes.

He chewed his salami club carefully, cracking whole peppercorns in his teeth. Then he returned to the office and retrieved Carney's drawings from the files. He taped them to his table, fighting off disappointment at what unfurled. The church was an elongated structure of masonry construction, just a sanctuary, basically, with a minister's office appended to one side. Green knew Carney's genius, and even in this minor building he could see it—how the narrowness of the sanctuary made it inevitable that parishioners' attention would be called to the altar, where Carney had specifications for a wooden overlay carved with LOVE NEVER FAILETH—but the church was flat-roofed, the windows standard and brick-silled, the exterior stucco on eight-inch cinderblock. What client would approve a design so severe?

Green considered the challenge ahead of him. A well-done perspective sold a layman on the beauty of a plan he would otherwise never comprehend. The problem with Carney's design was that its virtues were hidden inside. Viewed from a distance, in a perspective, the church would look like a long white shoebox. And Green knew it was important that Theo sell this plan. The city was in a building boom, but it was office buildings that were booming, downtown, where they could join the city's nascent skyline.

"Our little friend appears to be deep in contemplation," said Peter, one of the interns, a boy whose twiggy neck seemed inadequate for his head. Beside him was the third intern, Walter, mouth partly open. His allergies prevented him from breathing through his nose.

"Contemplating his head deep between Nancy's buttered breasts," Walter said. Both boys laughed sour laughs. The secretary never spoke to any of the interns. Probably exhausted, their theory went, from screwing every architect in the firm.

"I have a project," Green said. He tried to free his voice from inflection, but those two recognized pride and knew it was their duty to tamp it down.

"Well, well," Peter said, crowding Green to get a look at his table. "Carney put the touch on you. At long last."

"All hail the heir apparent," said Walter. "Maybe someday the Chosen One will throw us poor boys a bone."

Green knew he must change the subject quickly. When it came to mockery, their endurance was unsurpassed. He cast about for a new topic. Then he noticed Peter and Walter were wearing identical black ties.

"What's with the getups?" he asked.

Peter pulled his tie straight. "Adlai Stevenson's whistlestop pulls in tonight, after five. We're meeting the train."

"It's all planned," said Walter. "We've got the ties and dark glasses."

"And the twins loaned us their violin cases. We're going to wander the crowd carrying them. Like the criminal element, understand?"

"It'll be a hoot. You want to come?"

"I better not," said Green. "Carney needs this in two days."

Peter clasped his hands together, and, upon seeing him, Walter followed suit.

"Our prodigy," said Peter. "Tell me, have you ever been so proud?"

"Never," Walter replied, sniffing.

As they left, Green indulged a small hope that at the rally they'd get shot. He shook his head clear of it, then smoothed a clean sheet of vellum onto his board. He started a quick free-hand sketch, experimenting with different station points, trying to determine from which distance and angle the church would best appear. At five o'clock, he was still sketching, moving the sun around to change how the overhang might shade. Around him, the office folded up speedily, except for Carney, who remained hunched at his table, sweat staining the under-sleeve of his drawing arm. Green had to admire him, a man who worked so hard he was blind to day's end.

He decided to carry the plans and his sketches home and slid the rolled papers into a cardboard tube. On his way out, he would stop at the secretary's station, as the partners often did, to tell her when to expect him the next day.

Nancy was on the phone. Green lingered in front of her tidy desk, tapping the tube against his hip. She had grown plumper since the beginning of the summer, after the architects discovered her sweet tooth and started bringing in boxes of candy and quick breads their wives had baked. Most of the extra had gone to her chest, and when she tipped back in her chair, murmuring into the phone, the bodice of her dress strained and the spaces between buttonholes pinched open, to reveal—what? What miracle fabric could leave him so stirred?

Nancy covered the phone and asked impatiently, "What do you need?"

"I need the kind of woman," he said, surprising them both, "who gains her weight in the most womanly places."

Nancy's eyebrows lifted. Her lips, extravagant already, pursed into even fuller form. She glanced down at herself, then at him.

Green started to perspire. The tube he held felt like a club too large for his hand.

Smiling slyly, Nancy uncovered the mouthpiece and spoke into the phone. "Fine," she said. "We'll see about that."

Green had gone through all the beef his mother had left for him in the freezer and was now reduced to frozen sweets. For dinner he had half a loaf of zucchini bread, fudge with walnuts, three gumdrop cookies, and a slice of gooseberry pie. He uncapped a Coca-Cola and carried it down to the basement along with Carney's plans.

The light was dim. One of the basement's two bulbs was above his mother's sewing bench, where a half-finished dress lay trapped in the machine. For two weeks it had been there, since the afternoon her work had been interrupted by a phone call from Dr. Corn. Later that night, his parents had carried his brother to the car—by that time Roy couldn't walk—and the three of them had sped to the Infectious Diseases Hospital in

Chicago. His mother had grown up in the city, near the lake, and still retained her distrust of smaller towns and the abilities of those who lived there.

Green took a seat at the desk he'd set up beneath the basement's other bulb. In the past year he'd purchased a drafting board, a T-square, a set of triangles and French curves, five pencils of different weights, a large compass, and a vellum pad. Now he set the pop on the floor and used a soft cloth to wipe the T-square and the rest of the instruments and to dust erasure crumbs from the board. With his pocketknife, he dressed a 4H pencil to a conical point. He stroked a piece of paper into place and fixed the corners with tape. At last, he was ready to begin.

On his walk home he'd realized that landscaping would be his salvation. He would add a stand of oak trees near the entrance to soften and shade the church and a curved flower-lined path to offset the extremity of the building's lines. He pictured the family he'd include on the lawn: a stand-up father, his spotless wife, a well-fed junior in shiny brown shoes.

But now, clean page waiting, pencil dressed, he didn't make a mark. This was the best time, he thought, lingering in his perfect, completed vision, nothing on paper to remind him of what struggle lay ahead. He sat motionless, dreaming, unable even to start the picture plane. Then he summoned an image of Nancy standing behind him, pressing into his back, murmuring, *Yes, yes, perfect, exactly right.*

A ringing telephone roused him. Green left his table and sprinted up the stairs. It was his father, calling from the hospital.

"How is he?" Green asked.

"He's enjoying the whirlpool. They lower him in on a stretcher and soak him until his face turns bright red." His father halted for a moment to cough. "Your mother, however, is ready to sign him out and bring him home."

"Isn't he still contagious?"

"Right now they only let us see him through glass. But there's a shortage of nurses, so your mother volunteered to apply hot packs. She has to wear a mask and gloves, but today she saw him up close."

"So he is still contagious?"

"Roy told her he's been thinking about how different things would be if all the ceilings in our house were the floors. She thinks homesickness is confusing him." His father's breath came heavily. "The doctors are fighting her, but you know your mother. She's worried if Roy stays he'll end up in an iron lung."

Though his father's talk troubled him, Green couldn't bring himself to ask his question a third time. And in truth, he was fairly sure of the answer. McClain, a boy from school, had been in the hospital for over a month before he was released. His parents, Green guessed, were building castles in the air—they were aware that bringing his brother home sooner would be unsafe. But for three weeks they'd been sleeping in a noisy motel across the street from Roy's ward. Exhaustion had addled them into thinking their fantasies could be something real.

"I need you to gather the old army blankets in the garage, from Grandpa K's service," his father continued. "Cut them into strips, so they'll be ready to boil." He paused. "I'm sorry to say it, but you may need to quit your internship. It will require a great deal of effort to treat Roy at home."

"I should get off the phone now," Green said gently, not wanting to disrupt his father's dream. "I have an assignment for the firm."

"Good deal," said his father. "Mother sends her love. She says Roy looks forward to riding his bicycle with you very soon."

After hanging up, Green became aware of a deep pain in his shoulder. He'd worked enough for one day. True, he hadn't started the actual perspective, but he had considered it, both its form and content, and he believed in giving yourself credit for everything you do.

In the kitchen he poured himself a short shot of his father's whiskey before heading upstairs to draw a bath. With three capfuls of rose-scented bubbles, the water foamed sweetly. He undressed and stepped in with his drink. Naked and wet, whiskey melting his tongue, he closed his eyes and envisioned Nancy advancing in a black-skirted bathing suit, the front cut low and snug. She approached slowly, backed by a sun so strong he couldn't make out her face. No, that was wrong, her face was beautiful too, so he reworked the mirage, moving it to an indoor pool, the pool he had designed for his family, and now it was December, a foot of fresh snow piled outside. Nancy entered through the tiled portico he'd drawn, and while he watched, already soaking in the deep end, she leaned against a board-and-batten wall for balance as she removed her coat and unzipped her rubber boots. Smiling, she lifted her sweater over her head. Once it was off, he noticed how raw her cheeks were—from cold or wool, who could tell? Perhaps from modesty, as she spied the stretch of tall lancet windows spanning one wall. Not to worry, Green reassured her, those are custom-made, paned with special glass, allowing light in but blocking out sight. What he had gone through to track down that glass, studying dozens of design magazines, calling contractors in

California, writing a letter to the American Glass Manufacturers Board! Finally he had located a supplier able to produce the windows to his specifications, which Green had listed in a detail on a complete set of plans. Now, in his parents' tub, rose bubbles winking flat, he drifted into another fantasy, one in which he was bringing the bathhouse plans to work and showing the other interns or, better yet, Carney, explaining what great lengths he had gone to for a structure that had never been built. In the fantasy, Green was shaking his head, grinning, like he didn't understand his own foolish ways. But he did understand, and he was sure—now opening his eyes, now finishing his drink, now reaching back for the drain—that Carney would understand too.

"So right away Secret Service goons accost us, grab our violin cases, and lead us to a little trailer parked near the platform. Nothing in there but a card table and folding chairs, like somebody's expecting a nice poker game. One of the goons shoves us into chairs and the other one slams the cases on the table—all business—and flips the lids. But when he sees what's inside, I swear, the guy smiles. He takes out a violin, sticks the thing under his chin, and starts sawing the lousiest rendition of 'The Tennessee Waltz' you ever heard."

Peter, who was acting the drama while he spoke, nicked a pencil from Green's drafting table for a bow. Standing beside him, Walter watched appreciatively. Seated, Green strove to appear unimpressed.

"The other goon tells him to knock it off. So Mr. Music Maker stops, puts the violin in its case like he's putting down a baby, and comes around the table. He asks how old we are, and when we answer, he shakes his head and says, 'Boys, this is the time to think straight.' Then the other guy brings over a big box from the corner. The violin goon opens it and pulls out two cartons of Stevenson-for-President cigarettes. He says, 'Make the right choice, boys.' Then he gives us each a carton and lets us go."

"He let you go?" It wasn't the ending Green had been hoping for. He didn't like what the story suggested, that people who started off as assassins could wind up with free smokes.

"Don't be upset, brother." Peter threw a pack on the table. "We'll cut you in."

On the wrapper, Stevenson's face was awkward and cheerless, printed against a blue-starred flag. Green shook out a cigarette, and Walter, quick with the Zippo, provided light. The stick was low-grade and tasted like hay. Green smoked it anyway, and considered telling the story of his comment to Nancy about her weight. It would flatter him, yes, but once they heard it, Peter and Walter would demand he up the ante, and Green hadn't yet devised his next step. That morning he had come in the rear entrance so he wouldn't have to pass Nancy's desk.

He smoked, silent, the previous night's shoulder pain returning. When he twisted around to loosen the muscles, he saw Carney at his table sketching madly, the sun through the window spotlighting him like an insect on display.

Green lifted his shoe and snuffed the cigarette on the sole. "I have work to do," he announced.

Peter and Walter traded glances. Green ignored them. He had a project and he needed to complete it quickly, employing all his skills. He needed to make this perspective exceptional, to impress Carney and to lay the groundwork for an internship next summer, or for a part-time job during the school year.

He positioned a new sheet on his table and used a straight edge to draw the picture plane. He sketched in the plan view and fixed a station point. Then came the ground line, the right orthographic view, the eye-level horizon line, two vanishing points. He projected the plan view down to the ground line and flipped the right view over, all in light lead. Once he'd finished the basic outline of the church, he decided to start his landscaping, leaving the actual inking and shading of the structure for last. First the stand of oak trees, he decided, then the curved path, then the church-going family, those three happy nuts.

By noon he was still inking his first tree—after an extended internal debate, he'd decided that in the perspective the season was midsummer, when the trees would be fully leafed—but he stopped to perform his lunchtime duties, gathering orders and exiting through the back door for the walk to Andy's Eats. He walked leisurely, taking pleasure in his stride and the sun, until he thought of his brother flat in a hospital bed behind glass. Then he hurried to collect the lunches and return to the office, where, without thinking, he used the front door.

Nancy was eating a lunch brought from home: sliced tomato and a cold hamburger patty without bread.

"That looks good," he said.

"What looks good?"

"Your lunch."

She forked a tomato slice and lifted it. "Would you like some?"

"No, thanks."

"You don't need lunch?"

"I have my own." He raised one of the bags.

"I guess you don't need mine then." She sighed. "Too bad."

He remembered her red cheeks from his vision. The wool sweater lifted over her head.

"Autumn is coming," he said hopefully.

She leaned to see out the front door.

"No, not—" he stammered. "I mean, the summer is almost over."

Nancy regarded him archly. "It seems it isn't over quite yet."

He couldn't tell if she was signaling encouragement or disdain. He waited for more clues, but none were offered. She sliced her hamburger into quarters, then eighths.

"I guess I better deliver this food," he said.

Eighths became sixteenths. "Do what you need to," said Nancy.

Leaving her desk, he realized he didn't like her at all. But by the time he finished delivering most of the food, he'd recast their exchange as one between shy romantics, each wanting to express an emotion for which they did not have the words. That's it, he thought, kneeling to leave Carney's corned beef, that's exactly what we are!

"How is the perspective coming?"

Green raised his eyes to see Carney gazing down at him. The skin of his face hid his features in its folds.

"Terrific," Green said, standing. "Coming along fine."

"You'll have it done tomorrow morning?"

He hesitated for a moment. "Absolutely."

Carney's posture stiffened. He said, "Why don't I take a look."

Slightly nervous, Green led Theo to his table and whisked away the blank sheet protecting his work.

"What is this?" Carney asked immediately, his voice high. "Where is the church?"

"In the center." Viewing the sketch, Green could understand the confusion. It was difficult to spot the lightly penciled church. What stood out was the partial tree he'd drawn.

"You have no respect for me." Carney sounded bewildered. "I thought you had respect."

"I have a great deal of respect," Green assured him. "That why I'm incorporating additional design elements. To highlight the building's lines."

"To overshadow them, you mean?" Carney jabbed a finger at his original plan. "Each line here is a personal message to those in the trade. Each line is a risk I ask men to take."

Unnerved, Green spoke softly, hoping to pacify the architect. "That's true," he said. "And I would never even think of altering your elevations. But I though that since this is a perspective, for the client, I could take liberties."

Carney swallowed hard. "A man is in a foreign country with a friend," he began. "The man does not speak the language. His friend does. The man falls in love with a woman and asks his friend to translate a letter he's written to her. The friend takes liberties in his translation, makes it fancy. The woman reads the letter and thinks, All these flowers, all this poetry, where is love? She breaks with the man. As the friend watches, the now-destroyed man shatters a wine glass against the edge of the café table and uses a shard to open his veins." His neck flushed scarlet. "Tell me. Is that a true friend?"

"The friend probably thought he was helping the man," Green ventured.

"What man needs such help?" Carney shouted. "Tell me! What man?" He inhaled deeply, then used his sleeve to dry the sweat on his forehead. Again he pointed to his floor plan.

"This is in a language countless men have studied," he said more calmly. "If I sent this to a certain fellow in China, he would be able to comprehend." He unpeeled the tape at the plan's corners. "Tell me. Please. Why can't you?"

"I'll redo it," Green pleaded. "I have a drafting board at home. I'll work all night if I need to."

Carney began rolling the paper. "This is extremely important to me. I thought you knew."

"Sir, I'll work all night if necessary. I want to be a true friend!" Green was embarrassed to hear the phrase pass his lips, though it had been the right thing to say. Carney stopped rolling the sketch, and a tenderness overtook him, and it was a nice thing to see, Theo's face. But then his expression went funny, and Green realized—as Carney must have—that the office had quieted. The office watched, waiting for whatever came next.

Carney, stricken by the attention, nervously picked at his pockets, shirt, and pants, fingers fumbling, until he grabbed Green suddenly in a vigorous handshake.

"No tricks?" Carney said. "You will study the drawings? Listen to what they say?"

"Yes, sir." Green felt something pressed into his palm. When Carney released him, he saw what he had been given. In his hand was a pill, brilliant blue.

What a day! On his walk home, the windshield of a parked mail truck glittered like an ocean, choppy in the sun. Elated, he broke into a run, antsy to get to his desk before the elation disappeared. The phone was ringing as he rushed through his door, but he silenced it by ripping the cord from the wall.

At his drafting table, Green eagerly unrolled one of Carney's plans. When he bent over it, his joy ebbed away. Lines blurred into tangles that his eyes raced to straighten. He had hoped his mind had been sharpened to a point, but now it was painful, it was unbearable to concentrate.

Frustrated, he looked away from the paper to anywhere else, until his sight settled on his mother's sewing bench and her half-finished dress. It dawned on him that switching to another project—for a short while—might make it easier to focus on the perspective upon his return. He left the sketch and crossed the room to the machine. His mother had tutored him some, and once he had sewn her an apron, but when he studied the dress pattern, he couldn't make sense of the drawings or her notes. He despaired quickly but, a moment later, understood that his despair was misplaced. Even if he could complete the dress, his mother would never wear it. It would always recall to her Dr. Corn's phone call, the marker of when all their lives went wrong.

It was a shame, really, because the fabric was too fine to go to waste. He examined it closely, and as he ran it through his fingers, the very essence of that half-done dress began to change. It was no longer an unfinished dress, but an actual dress, just removed. When he closed his eyes, he saw Nancy lifting it over her flushed cheeks. But, he realized, to remove a dress, first you must be able to wear it. He vowed to finish the dress—not tonight, tonight was for other work—but some time in the future, after his mother came home and taught him more. Eyes still closed, he envisioned the final fitting: Nancy modeling, him pulling the fabric tighter, then tighter, fastening it, at last, with straight pins.

He felt his face and hands grow damp, and then he was too sweaty to return to his table. If he drew now, he would only smudge the lead. He refolded his mother's pattern and used it to fan himself. When he cooled, he could resume.

Why hadn't his parents let him build that pool? The city pools had been closed all summer, forcing him and Roy to spray each other with a hose on hot days. Until they heard about the secret creek behind McClain's house, where the South-of-Grand crew gathered to swim. Green and his brother biked over and ran through McClain's yard to the patch of woods out back. There, a group of boys swam in a slow, dung-smelling creek. His brother didn't want to, but Green shoved him and splashed in himself. They swam for one hour, then biked for two, trying to air the stink from their skin. That night, their mother made them take lemon baths. The next morning, when his brother tried to get out of bed, his legs wouldn't hold him and he fell to the floor.

Green stopped fanning himself and rushed to his table, where he found the bathhouse drawings in tubes underneath. A floor plan, side elevations, two perspectives he'd inked. There, in the top view, was the feature he sought—a small whirlpool, south of the shower. Roy was enjoying the whirlpool, his father had reported. Clearly, the time was right to reintroduce these designs. The challenge would be demonstrating to his parents the project's feasibility. His drawings proposed a lengthy, extensive transformation. But if he took the first step—clearing out the garage, chalking an outline of the pool—his parents might feel less threatened by the immensity of the plan.

He left the basement and the house for the garage. It was a free-standing frame structure with a gambrel roof and poured concrete floors. From its interior he dragged a croquet set to the driveway, before heading to a stretch of metal shelving against the rear wall. He removed a bucket of old tennis balls and a small toboggan, and then saw the stack of his grandfather's wool army blankets on the shelf above. Fond feelings came to him as he thought of his grandfather, who had built his own farmhouse and spent the rest of his life redoing its rooms. Then Green remembered his father's instructions: cut the blankets so they could be boiled for Roy. His parents were tired, he reminded himself. He should forgive their delusions. In the end, of course, reason would prevail. Still, the blankets would need to be cleared out before any remodeling could proceed.

He reached for a blanket and tugged. But an edge was wedged under the bowling ball case on the shelf beside it, and he flinched away as the case tottered and then crashed to the floor.

The impact left an ugly, ragged break in the concrete. He knelt over it, and when he checked the damage with his finger, more concrete chipped away. The thought came to him that with the proper tools he could really do some work on this floor. He could bring up most of it if there were enough of these cracks from which to begin. Dizzy with the idea, he pressed his cheek to the cool of the concrete. He had wanted to prove to his parents the transformation was possible. Better than drawings, he reasoned now, would be the actual breaking of ground.

He unzipped the ball's case and was surprised to find the ball was unhurt. He stood with the ball in his arms. When he dropped it again, the ball cracked, not the floor. Luckily, his grandfather had been a tournament bowler. There were a half dozen more in the garage. He lugged a stepladder to the metal shelf and climbed up for another ball, this one without a case. Starting down the ladder with it, it occurred to him that the original crack may have been the result of the greater height from which the first ball fell. He released the ball from where he stood on the ladder. This time the ball survived intact. Unfortunately, the concrete did as well.

Suddenly he remembered one of Grandpa K's projects: a remodel of an upstairs bedroom at the farm. His grandfather had installed a trap door in the bedroom floor that opened to the front porch below. Green and his brother had spent hours playing there, Green jumping through first, before Roy, who would lower himself halfway and then freeze. From the porch, Green would reach up to tickle his brother's thin ankles, until Roy, giggling, allowed himself to fall.

If he could drop a bowling ball through the roof of the garage, from that height, surely it would gather enough force to break the floor!

Green descended the ladder and zipped the second ball into the original ball's case. Then he used one of Grandpa K's blankets to fashion a sling, first working the blanket through the curved handle of the bag. With a pair of gardening shears he split the blanket's corners and twisted the split pieces into a bulky knot. He slipped the tied knot over his head, arranging the blanket across his chest like a sling and then placing the ball inside. The ball's weight pulled the knot against his throat and made his breath short, but the blanket held and left his hands free. On a wall he found one of his father's hammers and hung it on his belt loop. Now he was ready to climb.

Outside, an oak tree overhung the garage, its low branches solid and thick. Green reached for one and planted his foot against the trunk. When he lifted himself, his heart throbbed wildly, and he paused on the next branch, waiting to find his breath before moving on. He climbed intently, stopping often, until finally he was level with the roof. Balancing the case on a branch and inching it ahead of him, he shimmied over the leaf-choked rain gutter and above the garage. From there, he assessed the roof's slant. It was low-pitched. No reason to be afraid to let go.

He hit the roof hard. With the ball dragging him, he had to scrabble desperately to halt his slide. His feet struck the gutter and knocked a section free. But it stopped him, and he was able to crawl up to the level ridge between the roof's two slopes. Panting, he wriggled out of the sling and set the ball beside him. Then he sprawled on the shingles, taking in the black sky. He saw then the sky was one flat surface. The sky revealed to him everything it had.

He raised himself to a crouch and attacked the shingles. With the hammer, they came up as easily as tape. It confirmed the rightness of what he was doing. The roof was garbage anyway and should be replaced.

As Green worked, night changed into morning, so gradually it kept him unaware. Some time later he missed the sound of an automobile turning into the driveway. By then, he'd stripped a good patch of shingles and was destroying the tongue-and-groove sheathing underneath. Only when a horn blared did he pause and peer over the roof edge. A familiar station wagon was parked on the gravel, his father beside it, head tipped back to peer up at him.

Green called out, to direct his father into the garage, where he could explain what he'd done and his future plans. But he went silent when he spotted the mattress stuffed into the wagon, his sick brother on top, smothered in quilts. A sensation engulfed him—not love, not welcome—but a thick, black, greasy heat that bled from his heart like hot tar.

Why?

He had been spared once.

Why would they risk him again?

Below, his father removed his hat. His mother stepped from the car, shielding her eyes against the day.

It was impossible. He laid down the hammer in a brume of insulation and hoisted the bowling ball from its case and overhead.

First he would warn them.

"Don't come closer!" Green screamed. "Stop right there!"

US, CRAZY

It was past midnight when Lucy pulled back the examination curtain and saw an underweight woman with red hands sitting on the edge of the bed.

"Doctor, they burn," the patient cried.

It turned out the woman had chopped a hundred jalapeño peppers earlier in the evening, commanded to by her cracked vision of God. Lucy prescribed topical lotion and a good hand washing and moved to the next curtain, where there was a bleeding man who had shaved half his head because some of the hair on it didn't belong to him. His eyeballs were loose and full of veins, and when Lucy questioned him, he admitted he'd been on a meth bender and hadn't slept in three days. "The Language says sleep is a thief," he told her sadly. "The Language says rob the thief before the thief robs from you."

Lucy had a nurse clean him up while she sneaked out of the emergency room to the dock for a cigarette. She paced, ignoring the stars, smoking fast so she could get back inside. She loved her work. Doctoring had made her strong and deliberate, even in disaster's midst. Last winter, snowed in at the airport in New York, she'd removed the stitches in some guy's ass with her Swiss Army knife. The waiting area had burst into applause.

Just as she was finishing her cigarette, Kristi, a fellow intern, came out to the dock tapping a pack on her palm. She moved like a dancer and wore strung around her neck a collection of nut-sized protective charms. She was heavily involved in voodoo, and once Lucy had gone with her to a service held in the attic of a bright Queen Anne home near West Des Moines. She'd gone without preconceptions, ready to transcend the everyday, but when the service started she saw it wasn't for her. The priestess seemed too dependent on props.

Kristi never held it against her. "Hey, chick," she said now, wrapping an arm around Lucy's waist and squeezing. "They're paging your sweet self inside."

Lucy thanked her and cursed her crappy beeper and headed to the bank of phones near the intake desk. When she got through to the switchboard, an operator gave her a name and a number that was from out of town. It was Martha, her father's ex-lover, a Zoroastrian scholar who'd recently ended the affair. Martha had decided to focus on her new husband, a Chinese Religions specialist whose translation of the *I Ching*—Lucy's father had complained to her bitterly—was a critical and popular success.

"I'm sorry to bother you," Martha started when Lucy reached her, "and let me assure you right off the bat that for now I'm not calling the police. But I wanted to let someone who cared about him know exactly what is going on."

She has the voice of a professor, Lucy thought, seductive and indiscriminately amused.

"Your father is not handling the situation well," Martha pressed on. "He's sending me three faxes a day, wherever I am. In Florence, last week, there was one waiting at the villa. He's sent several faxes addressed to me in care of conference chairs, posing as an old boyfriend with HIV, informing me of his status so I can get tested too. He somehow got in touch with a grad student here and convinced her to transcribe one of my lectures, and then wrote me a letter as if he'd attended the lecture, quoting me, and said I probably didn't recognize him because he's suffering from a wasting illness and now wears the face of death."

"How long has this been happening?" Lucy asked.

"The past several weeks. My husband wants me to go to the police, but I haven't. I don't fear your father. Who could? But I'm afraid he might harm himself."

Who could? It seemed an unnecessary slur. "I'm seeing him later today," Lucy said. "I'll talk to him about it. I'm sorry for the trouble he's putting you through." The apology felt strange in her mouth, offered to the woman who had wrecked her home. "Since I have your number," she made herself continue, "maybe I should check in soon to see if he stops."

There was silence. Lucy listened to Martha breathe. "That would be fine," the other woman said finally, 'but please, please don't pass my number to him."

"I'm sure I wouldn't," Lucy said.

She hung up, and then there was a commotion in the waiting room. A woman in a wedding dress charged through the automatic door, wailing and nursing a newborn child. Leaning against the wall by the phone bank, Lucy, for a moment, closed her eyes. Her father had called earlier in her shift and in a thick voice asked her to breakfast at the lunch counter in Hy-Vee. He sounded upset, but wasn't that to be expected? He and Martha had been carrying on a long-distance affair for almost twenty years. They had called each other at noon and at midnight and taken exotic vacations during academic breaks. When Lucy was nine, her father had sent her a photo of him and Martha standing side by side on an Ecuadorian beach. Both were sunburned and wild-eyed, and studying the photo at night always had aroused a thrill in Lucy's belly that kept her from sleep. June, her most recent therapist, was very interested in Lucy's reaction. June theorized it was the sight of her father with an unfamiliar woman that had disturbed her younger self. But in Lucy's memory, she'd been picking up some hot, inscrutable feeling that came off that photograph like steam. She tried to explain it to June by recalling what her father had written on the back of the photo: *Us, crazy.* "You were only nine," June responded with a frown.

Lucy's boyfriend, Biard, was the ob/gyn intern on call that night. She expected him to be napping, but when she walked into the call room he was propped in the lounge's butterfly chair, reading *Ecce Homo,* too absorbed to hear her come in. She stood at the door, observing the carelessness of his posture, the length of his neck, the tension he held near his eyes.

"I don't think the hospital basement in the middle of the night is a safe place to read Nietzsche," she said. "Better to read him in the park, while you're at a family picnic or something."

He rested the book on his chest and gazed skyward. "*In the end one loves one's desire and not what is desired.*"

She knew Nietzsche only by reputation, so she changed the subject. "Why aren't you asleep?"

"I pissed off a nurse earlier, and now she's punishing me." He pressed his fingers to his forehead. "She keeps calling with questions like, is it all right if she gives Mrs. Whoever a sponge bath? When I lie down again, I'm too tense, just waiting for her next stupid call."

"Sometimes when I can't sleep," said Lucy, "I imagine myself as a dying patient, fading in and out, but somehow aware that all the people I love are at my bedside, remarking on my beauty."

"Really," Biard said.

"Or I'm an injured girl who's being carried on a stretcher, all wrapped in furs and blankets, through a blizzard in some far-off place."

She affected a dreamy pose, all the while watching to see if she was achieving the right effect: whimsical, in an intriguing but not mawkish way. Their relationship was still in its Age of Enchantment, but she knew she'd have to work to make it last. When they had first met, Biard had explained he found monogamy difficult, and she had known then, even as she took another sip of her gimlet, he was confessing it so that later, when he did cheat, he could shrug and say matter-of-factly, "Buyer beware."

"So I got this disturbing phone call," she said. "Apparently my father has been totally stalking this old lover of his."

"How are you doing with that?" She recognized the flatness that came into his voice. They'd both been trained in the developmental helping model of counseling. They both knew to ask questions that couldn't be answered *yes* or *no.*

"I almost can't stand to think about it. Lately, when I see him in person, I have a hard time looking directly at his face. He looks so *old.*" She heard her voice catching and swallowed to stop.

Biard didn't respond, so she kept talking.

"You know, there was this guy who stalked me my last year of med school."

"You don't say," Biard said.

"I met this sophomore at a party and brought him home. He left early in the morning, and I thought I'd never see him again, but he started calling ten times a day, saying things like he was at a dealership buying me a Jeep. Finally he calls from the hospital and accuses me of ratting him out to his parents and getting him committed. Which was ironic, because I hadn't done anything. In fact, my friends were mad at me because I wouldn't call the police."

"You got off on the whole insane Romeo scene."

"No," Lucy insisted. "I was scared that if I did anything, if I actually acknowledged his behavior as threatening, he'd suddenly see himself in that light and be compelled to act out that role."

"Admit you loved it," Biard said.

"I was scared," Lucy said. "Later on, he sent me his watch in the mail, from the hospital. I did wear it for a while. It was huge. It made my wrist look petite."

"Check her out," Biard said, smirking. "She drives us men mad."

"That wasn't my point," she said, though she supposed on some level that's why she'd told the story. But the truth was the poor kid had been a time bomb, and it was chance she had happened to rub up against him right as his bipolar disorder made itself known.

"Hey, nothing big, no need to deny it," Biard said. "You're a very self-absorbed girl. And about three-quarters of that narcissism is affirming and useful. It's just the other 25 percent that's sad and sick."

"Quit," she said. "You're swelling my head."

"But it's that other 25 percent that keeps me interested," Biard said. Then he reached into the pockets of his coat and brought back a small clear vial and an empty syringe. It was all the rage at the General. The interns liked to shoot up magnesium on their overnight calls.

Lucy slipped out of her coat and removed her shirt and balanced on Biard's knee. He was an expert—there was just a tiny pinch before her body flooded with heat. She rose and did a shivery little dance that took her across the room. From there, she admired Biard as he shot himself up. He was gorgeous. He ran triathlons and baked bread and wrote trippy little children's songs. The boy could sew his own clothes, for Christ's sake!

Biard dropped the syringe and slumped in his chair, deep in the magnesium glow. "If only I could stick corks in all these women's vaginas and sleep straight through the night."

"Yeah," she said. "Sounds good."

He gave her a look. "Come here."

She went. He pulled her to him, and then they were rushing through a series of motions that were not altogether delineated, until suddenly she was straddling him on the chair. For a few breaths, she slipped into something like pleasure, but then caught sign of a bruise on her thigh and got lost in summoning back to her memory its cause. When she returned, Biard was moaning into her neck, and she became aware of the complicated rhythm in the room. She eased into the swing of it. It was really very good.

"Now tell me I'm beautiful," she said after they finished. "Better yet, tell me all other women are ugly."

"They're horrible," he said, lifting her off him. He reached for his pants. "There's Mrs. Whoever in the birthing room, screaming for drugs when she's barely dilated. I was trying to get her to visualize a peaceful scene, but she wasn't having it. I'm like, 'Why don't you try watching your breath?' But no."

"She's got to do it her way," Lucy chided. "It's not your birth." She stood before him, buttoning her shirt.

"Not yet," he said and gave her belly a kiss. She put on a faint smile, but she knew it was bullshit, like their plans to buy a coffee farm in South Kona or spend a year hiking the Appalachian Trail. Still, there was a part of her that resisted her own intuition and believed that it could, in the end, work out fine. In any case, she had secretly stopped the Pill, with vague notions whirling in her head about postponing his inevitable goodbye. Yeah, it was sneaky and manipulative, but she told herself it was for the greater good—hers and his and what would surely be one nice-looking kid.

"It seems to me," she said, straightening her coat, "it's better if your motivations are pure, but even if they're impure, as long as they motivate you and spur you to action, you can work on purifying them later on."

"Are you thinking about your father?" said Biard.

"Sure," she said.

"So what are you going to do?"

Lucy settled into his lap. "I'll see if I can get him to have some insight into his own behavior so he can better apprehend the reality of the situation. He's prone to magical thinking. I'll see if I can break through that."

"You're a good girl," Biard said. "You're a very smart girl."

She leaned into his chest as he described the Thai meal he'd cook that night, and pondered which Miles Davis CD to bring over, and related some of the ideas he'd been having about fractals and lucid dreams.

At seven in the morning, Lucy left the hospital to meet her father. The lunch counter was right inside the Hy-Vee entrance, and Lucy found a stool and ordered a short stack and peppermint tea. An elderly couple next to her placed their order and asked for two empty glasses. When the waitress returned and set the glasses on the counter, the old woman pulled a jar filled with milk from her purse and poured. Lucy regarded the couple tenderly. They reminded her of her grandparents, who, on family road trips to Colorado, would sit in the car and eat cheese and grape jelly sandwiches while Lucy and her mother went into McDonald's and ordered burgers and fries.

She was plotting how the conversation with her father might go—she'd let him introduce the subject of Martha and wait to see what he disclosed, unasked—when he appeared at the entrance to the store. His expression was one of mild confusion, though not enough, she thought, to arouse pity or alarm. Watching her father scan the room, Lucy suddenly wished she had taken a shower. She felt grimy. Around him, she became a stranger to herself.

"Dad," she called.

Her father crossed the room and took the stool next to hers

and set his bag on the floor. He ordered three soft scrambled eggs and coffee, and then turned and said, "What's going on in your life?"

On June's advice, Lucy had once pointed out to her father how he monopolized their conversations and never asked about her. Since then he made a big show of letting her talk first. She often wished she'd never brought it up.

"For instance," her father said, grasping for a topic, "how's therapy?"

"Therapy," Lucy said. "Actually last session June came up with something interesting." Even as she chose her words she saw how what June told her might spark something in him. "June said I'm like a person with a big bowl of candy. And when I meet someone, before I even get to know them, I dump the whole bowl in their lap, like 'Here, I want you to have it all.'"

The waitress poured her father a cup of coffee. He stuck his finger in to check the heat.

"So then the person realizes that me giving them the candy isn't about any genuine feeling I have for them. It's more about an obsessive desire to give it all away to somebody. To have anybody else take it. And that's not particularly attractive, right? So June suggested I don't lavish my candy on someone right away. Make the other person earn it, one piece at a time."

"Sounds like game-playing to me," her father said.

"It's not a game. It's about being self-aware."

"Sounds calculating," her father said. "And the metaphor? Whew. A stretch."

The waitress brought more coffee and Lucy's stack of pancakes, and Lucy cursed the knob of butter she'd forgotten to ask for on the side. She originally had mixed feelings about the candy metaphor too—just the word *candy* made it seem dumb—but then the image had appeared in her mind a few times when she was with Biard and helped her maintain discipline. But this discussion was not supposed to be about her.

She poured syrup on her cakes. She asked her father how his research project was going. After years of skipping from specialty to specialty, and failing to build a publication record that might propel him beyond the survey course he taught at the community college, in the last year he'd started a serious study of the Southeast Asian religious diaspora, focusing on the relocation of Lao Buddhists to Des Moines.

"That's not my project anymore," her father said, light coming into his face. "Now I'm onto Sufism. I go to Chicago every few weeks to meet with a sheikh and a group of dervishes and participate in the Remembrance of God. We chant a selection of God's ninety-nine names, and read Rumi, and dance, and praise love."

"Isn't Rumi a bit trendy these days?" she said, deciding to be snotty. "Isn't he like the new Kahlil Gibran?"

Her father cleared his throat. "*Hail to thee, O Love, sweet madness! Thou who healest all our infirmities! Who art the physician of our pride and self-conceit!*"

He spoke in a different voice when he quoted someone else, more respectful of their words than his own. He looked at her expectantly. She knew what he wanted. He wanted to be recognized as a man made sick by his enormous capacity for love. But she wouldn't do it.

"Martha contacted me at the hospital last night," Lucy said. "She told me the kinds of things you've been doing to harass her. She's considering calling the police."

Her father's face changed. He studied his flatware on the counter. "*I'm* the one who's done something criminal?" he said, softer. "Who's the one who's caused the most harm?" He rested his fork on his spoon. "I should have seen it coming, I suppose. Those Zoroastrians cling to their vicious creation myth. An original plant, an original bull, a First Man, and what do the gods do but kill them all and scatter their remains? Yes, the idea being that new plants and bulls and men spring forth, but tell me, what kind of person adheres to an origin tale like that?"

"Maybe you can use that to help you let her go," Lucy said. "The fact that you two don't really subscribe to the same worldview."

"I was trying to be glib, Lucy. Couldn't you tell from my tone?" Her father lifted his coffee, but left it unsipped. "No, of course not, you're still a sweet kid." His voice held no affection. "Don't you ever play around with love. Love is a gun."

"I know what love is," she said.

"Love is a sock stuffed in your mouth," he said, putting his cup down. "No, that's not it either. How can I explain? It's like the impossibility of describing to you what the guanabana fruit tastes like. You've never even traveled to the Southern Hemisphere."

"Dad, I know what love is."

"Look," he said. "It's like this. Before I met Martha, when I was with your mother, there was a fixed set of emotions I regularly experienced, and, in a sense, those emotions did deviate greatly from each other, if you can imagine plotting them along some sort of emotional spectrum, with, say, positive and negative poles. In other words: sometimes I felt happy. Sometimes I felt sad. But the total number of my emotions was quite few.

I wasn't affectless, if you see what I mean, but my repertoire was limited. There was no depth on the bench."

The waitress offered him a plate of eggs.

"But with Martha, the breadth of human experience opened up to me. There are so many different ways to feel. Look, I have something to show you, something to help you understand." He bent to his bag on the floor.

"I know what love is," Lucy said again. "I'm actually involved in a very nuanced relationship." But he wasn't hearing her.

Her father handed her a spiral notebook with a bent-up cover and pages gray and soft. She opened to the first page, which was covered in a thick scrawl that occasionally resolved into words. It was a list, with a few legible entries.

> *3. a diffuse incredulity at world's wonders . . . 7. magnanimity unbounded by desire for personal gain . . . 16. most juicy sense of well being (1.23.96).*

"Understand?" her father said. It sounded like he was holding his breath as he spoke, and when she looked, his face was dull red. When she shook her head, he continued.

"I'm in the process of cataloging all the emotions I experienced in the seventeen years I was with Martha. It's quite an extraordinary process, really, recollecting these things which are conventionally viewed as intangible affective states and compiling them into hard evidence of love's power to transport us beyond the limits of what we thought we could perceive."

Lucy flipped to the middle of the notebook.

> *155. eerie, half-aborted pain (mostly at night) . . . 167. judicious inclinations toward ambition . . . 173. complete lack of guile . . . 181. BLISS, BLISS, BLISS!*

Her heart worked like a hammer. Martha had been wrong. Her father could inspire fear.

"You do see why I can't stop now," her father said.

"This is why you called me to meet you?" Lucy asked.

She wasn't expecting his reaction, the new dread that took over his face. "Oh," he said. "Wait. I forgot. I got carried away." He put his head in his hands, and when he raised it again, his cheeks were streaked with tears. "I've found a lump," he said. "I think I have cancer of the breast." Then he was struggling to lift his shirt over his head.

It was a nightmare.

"Not here, Dad, not here," Lucy said. "It's unlikely you have breast cancer, but I can give you an exam when we get home." She pulled his shirt down, left money on the counter, and took his arm to lead him to her car in the lot. As she helped him into the passenger seat, her mind zoomed through its implanted algorithms: maybe depression, triggered by chemical imbalance and recent emotional trauma, manifesting as somatic illness, probably best addressed, at this stage, with cognitive therapy and the standard drug protocol. She'd take him to the hospital for an evaluation, and get some Valium in his blood to calm him down.

"Please," her father said before she could start the engine. "Now that I've remembered I can't wait any more."

"That's fine," she said. Soothe him, strip away his delusions one by one.

She helped him remove his shirt. Her father smelled like a forest, and over the years, he'd become a puffier man. She had him put his hand on his head, and then she palpated his chest. She considered pretending to feel a lump, to shoot him out of his obsession with Martha. But she didn't feel anything even close.

"Where do you think this lump is?" she asked.

He took her hand and moved it to a ridge in his armpit.

"That's your pectoralis muscle," Lucy said. She put his fingers under his own arm. "Feel here on the other side. It's exactly the same."

"It's not the same," he said.

"Trust me. It's the same." Lucy, hurt that even in this he doubted her, removed her hand. "You must not send Martha any more faxes about HIV," she said, speaking in the clearest, flattest voice she could find. "If you do, she's going to take legal action. You probably will lose your job."

Her father pulled his shirt around his shoulders. "I shouldn't have brought you into this," he said. "This is my business. It is not your concern."

"I've made it my business," Lucy said. "I'll be checking in with Martha to make sure you leave her alone."

He stopped everything. "You have her phone number?"

"Forget it, Dad."

"I need that number," he said. "There's a certain resonance in my voice."

"Are you that far gone?" she said, frustrated. "Do you think I'm going to enable you to stalk her more?"

Her father lowered the visor mirror and considered his eyebrows. "*Those who are not fishes are soon tired of water*," he said. "*They who lack daily bread find the day very long.*"

"Dad."

"*The Raw comprehend not the state of the Ripe.*" Still gazing at the mirror, her father slapped some color into his cheeks and tucked in his shirt. "I never should have showed you my note-book," he informed her coolly. He opened the car door. "You're no intellectual," he said. "You never were an intellectual."

"Dad," she said. "I'm a very smart girl."

Her father stepped out and started through the lot, dodging cars. Observing him, Lucy suddenly saw how his world was a minefield. She got out and followed him, asking that he please not leave. She said harm coming to him was the scariest thing either of them could think of, so why not work together to make sure he was fine. She asked to see his notebook again. She said she knew he'd been wrecked by the vastness of his love. She even promised to give him Martha's number, but he must have known she was lying, because he ran to his car and locked the doors.

Lucy watched as her father drove away. In his car's wake, the pavement warped, an illusion she chalked up to sleep deprivation and the heat. She hadn't been outside much lately, and she squinted in the sun. Above, in the trees circling the lot, the seventeen-year cicadas cried and cried. A memory returned from the last time the cicadas had emerged—the summer her father left them, the summer her mother became afraid of the rhubarb stalks growing wild in the backyard. A friend had arrived to take her mother to the hospital, and Lucy hovered at the car door, asking her mother why she had to go. Her mother tried to hold it together, but the cicadas were relentless, and Lucy kept asking questions, and finally her mother stopped pretending and screamed, "Leave me the fuck alone!" Even then, her mother sobbing in the backseat, Lucy let herself have a quick fantasy in which she was the one going away to be placed under a doctor's care. Seeing her mother head to the hospital, she had wished to be in her place.

Now Lucy stood alone in the parking lot, sweaty, boxed in by the cicadas' droning song. She was stupid, but even she knew what came next. The adults would die. Then the nymphs would fall to the ground and start digging, impatient for their dark years to begin.

WONDERLAND OF ROCKS

Green sat in the rock garden outside his parents' apartment in Cathedral City and considered the mountains. They ringed the desert at a distance, bracing the yellow sky. They aroused in him thoughts of things large and undone.

"I think I prefer an open horizon," Green said to his wife.

Nora rose from her lounge chair and posed, hands on hips, surveying the range. Over her swimsuit she wore a thin pink T-shirt from the shop his father had opened after moving to California. She had wet it in the sink before putting it on, and the sun had shrunk the cloth to her form. Green appreciated it. They'd been married for less than a year.

"I like a horizon with a lot going on," she said after a moment. "It gives your eyes something to do."

It was Nora's first trip to California, Green reminded himself. It was understandable the desert had made her a fool. No help that his brother Roy had been plying her with weed all week, and with stories about the Cahuilla who used to live on the valley floor. Green took a drink from the weak margarita his mother had mixed him. She'd been free with the lime, and after a swallow, his mouth went dry.

His brother bounded through the sliding door onto the patio, dressed in a P.S. I LOVE YOU T-shirt and jeans cut off at the knee. Childhood polio had left one of his legs skinny and short.

"Packs are packed," Roy announced. "Let's hit the road."

Green drained the margarita. He wanted another.

"This guy at the motel hooked me up with some 'shrooms," Roy continued. "He cooked them in honey so they'll be easy to get down."

"I don't know," Nora said. She adjusted the bottom of her suit. "I get real superior when I'm tripping. People start looking ugly. I can't stand to see them eat."

"We'll be camping solo at first," Roy assured her. "You won't see any people. You can hang in the sand and do your own thing."

"What about coyotes?" Green said. "What about mountain cats?"

"What are you crying for, man?" Roy said.

"These mountains don't put me at ease," said Green. Taking his glass, he stood and slipped past the two of them into the cool of the shuttered apartment where his father was recuperating from a heart attack he'd suffered two weeks before. Green, Nora, and Roy had flown in from Des Moines after it happened. They would return to Iowa—they thought—soon.

It took a moment for his eyes to adjust, and then he saw his father on the couch, idly spinning the desk globe Green and Roy had given him when he retired out west. His father's hair had faded to the color of peanut shells. Green sat beside him. From the kitchen he heard a blender whirl.

"We're going to go," Green said. "We'll be back Sunday."

His father nodded. "Your little brother needs a few days to work on his perspective," he said. Yesterday there had been a fight that ended with Roy yelling, "Where's your generosity of spirit?" and his father throwing a glass.

"It's all right we go?"

His father had a tight smile. "You're asking if I'm going to kick off while you're gone?"

"I would never ask you that," Green said.

"Rest assured," said his father, "you'll know if I do."

After the first heart attack, when Green was in high school, some evenings his father was hit with chest pain so severe he'd get out of bed and spend the night in the living room recliner. Green would lie in his own room and pay attention to his father's heavy breath coming and going, until he mixed it up with his own breath and fell asleep. In the morning he'd wake with a start, afraid his father was dead in the chair.

His father looked through the glass door to the rockery, where Nora and Roy were still taking the sun.

"Bring me some white sage if you find some on the ground," his father said absently. "I need to give this place a good smudge."

His mother arrived with a blender of margaritas and refilled Green's glass. She settled into the couch between him and his father. Her presence soothed Green a bit. His feelings for her were clear and straightforward, and he knew hers for him were the same.

"Those mountains," she said with a sigh.

Smog from Los Angeles blew into the valley through the San Gorgonio Pass.

Green rode in the front of the car with his mother. Roy and Nora studied topographical maps of Joshua Tree in the back. As they merged onto the highway, a man on a bicycle pedaled onto the shoulder, guiding an empty bicycle beside him with his palm on the seat.

"It's OK we're leaving?" Green asked his mother. Her face was flushed from the morning's drinks.

"You're too hard on yourself," she said. "This trip will be good for everyone. Your father needs a more peaceful atmosphere. Roy will get a chance to cool down." Her hands on the wheel were thickly veined.

In the back, Roy was trying to impress Nora with trivia he'd picked up from their father's guidebooks.

"There's a lizard who spends his whole life in a Joshua tree," he said. "Born there, dies there. Feet never even touch the ground."

Green glanced at Nora in the rearview mirror. She chewed on her thumb, affecting to care.

"Not like most lizards," Roy went on. "Most lizards hit the ground running. They're born knowing someone's out to eat them. They're scared from the start."

"So you're saying there's actually more than one type of lizard," Nora said. The thought came to Green that she and Roy had smoked something before they started the drive.

"Remember those lizards, Green," his brother instructed. "Remember: don't lose your honor through fear."

"What did you say?" He turned quickly in his seat. Roy favored him with a sly smile.

"He's making the lizard stuff into a metaphor," Nora explained.

"Girl," his mother chided, not taking her eyes off the road, "don't encourage them."

"A lizard's brain is stamped with fear. In big letters: FEAR! Not for one moment are they free."

"It's sad," Nora said, shaking her head.

"Green is afraid to go camping," said Roy. "He's scared Tahquitz is going to find him and eat up his soul."

"You peg-legged bastard." Green tried to make his tone light. "Where's your generosity of spirit, huh? Is that something you can explain?" He wondered where Roy and Nora had managed to smoke and when they had found the time.

"Tahquitz has an evil visage," said Roy. "He's got an arrow stuck straight through his head."

"Hush now," his mother said wearily. "Why don't all of you be quiet and stare out the windows for a while."

There was scrub brush and sand on either side of the highway, and strings of low wooden-faced buildings, baked white in the sun. A school bus had stalled, and a group of kids, slick with heat, stood in a trough just off the road. They waved weakly to Green as he passed. He raised a hand. A new smell came off him. He swallowed and tasted dust in his throat.

After turning into the park, they drove to the Croc Rocks area, where Roy directed his mother to stop. They would hike from there to the base of Queen Mountain, a modest rise about a mile away.

Green unloaded the bags from the trunk. The sky was unclouded and full of glare.

"The Mormons entered the desert, thirsty as hell, and then the rain came!" Roy announced. He shouldered his pack and swayed under the weight of all the water inside.

"Take it easy," his mother said. "Be good." She helped Roy adjust his straps.

"One of the Mormons fell to his knees and cried, 'These trees welcome us into the desert like Joshua!'"

"Keep an eye on him," his mother told Green. "And don't worry. We'll see you in a couple of days."

He hugged his mother, and so did Nora, and when she let go, his mother's face was glassy in the light. She started the car, and as she drove away, he could see where someone had traced WASH ME into the rear window's dirt.

Roy shook his fist in the air. "Like Joshua!"

"Joshua was at Jericho, right?" Nora said. "Or did I switch him with somebody else? I always get him and Jacob mixed up."

"You're right," Roy said. "Absolutely right."

They set off into a stretch of desert, Roy in the lead with his fast, crooked stride, Green next, Nora bringing up the rear.

After a few silent minutes, Green stopped at a dyeweed bush and crumbled a sprig between his fingers. He watched Nora as she took a rise, bent forward at the waist, eyes on her own feet. When she arrived at the bush, her forehead was wet. He raised his fingers for her to smell.

"The Cahuilla mixed this into a deodorant paste to use when they hunted deer," he said.

Nora's face went sweet. "I sometimes forget you know things I don't," she said.

"I'll teach you," he said, joking.

"Teach me," she said, and for a moment it was like she was offering up a tender spot on her body. And him there with a bow in his hand.

"So you and Roy smoked earlier?" he said with what he hoped was nonchalance.

Nora fixed him with a look. "You don't need to feel threatened," she said. "He doesn't have anything you don't."

It seemed a strange leap for her to make. Roy stopped ahead and waited impatiently, stomping his boots.

Green pulled Nora to him and opened her mouth with his tongue. He ran a hand over her chest and down the front of her shorts.

"Gosh, thanks," she said when he let go. "That felt really sincere."

She moved past him, and Green followed her and Roy through an expanse of chollas and wait-a-minute thorn bushes until they descended into a sandy wash to the south of Queen Mountain and dropped their packs. Roy tied a tarp to a wind-crippled Joshua tree and staked it out at three points. Green set up his stove and started a pot of water to boil.

"Let's eat them up," he said, taking charge.

Nora spread thick smears of peanut butter on three slices of bread and then gave them to Roy, who unknotted a plastic bag and laid a few honey-soaked mushrooms on top of each slice. They ate the sandwiches quickly, then Green fixed rice and beans rolled in tortillas. He held the food in his mouth for a while in an effort to mask the 'shroom taste.

"So when's it going to hit me?" Nora asked.

"Takes a while," Green said, chewing. "It's probably hit once we're on solo."

"I'm not nervous about being solo the rest of today," Nora said, "But I'm nervous about solo all night."

"Not to worry," said Roy. "There's only one thing to keep in mind: if you sleep, don't sleep with your head to the east."

"Why not?"

"East is the direction Death takes on his way to Telmekish." Roy started talking about the two moving hills that guard Telmekish, and how the hills part if you've lived a good life or crush you if you've done wrong. Green listened, annoyed. It infuriated him how Roy stole other people's myths for his own kicks. Their father had bought them a book of Cahuilla tales when they visited the desert as kids, and back in Des Moines, Green and Roy had read it obsessively, imagining themselves into the book. But they weren't kids anymore.

"You're a boring white boy with no stories of your own," he interrupted.

"You don't know what color runs through these veins," Roy said calmly.

"What, now you're Native?"

"I say: your father and my father may not be the same man."

"You're so full of shit."

"I say: our mother may have drunk from other faucets." Roy brought his hands together in prayer position and bowed his head. "And I say: nothing more."

"Nothing more," echoed Nora.

"Let's go," Green said, getting to his feet, wanting now to be free of them both.

They lifted their packs and walked away from the camp. Roy

chose his solo spot first, on a small swell by a date palm. He unrolled his sleeping pad and lay flat. Nora and Green continued walking until she stopped at a hollow the size of a kid's swimming pool, where a cluster of Indian paintbrush grew.

"I guess this spot is good for me," she said.

"All right," Green said. "But don't hike out from here on your own. If you hurt yourself, we wouldn't know where to look."

"I don't believe that," she said.

There was a tiny silver whistle attached to his sport knife, and he detached it and gave it to her. "If you get to feeling uneasy," he said. "I'll be within earshot."

She slid the whistle into her pocket and waited for him to walk away. Suddenly he didn't want to leave. For whatever it was worth, she had chosen him. Who else had ever done that?

"Sorry about before," he said. "The kiss. I don't know why I did it."

"You do too," she said and smiled, her expression distant and moony.

Green had socked away an extra burrito—it had the weight and form of a baby's arm—and he ate it camped on the desert floor. "You'll know if I do," his father had told him, and he hoped the 'shrooms would make his senses fine enough to perceive that and more. But as he ate, nothing came to mind. He sank into a memory in which Nora walked across their bedroom in Des Moines naked, as slow and deliberate as a goose. She was bringing him a daisy, one she'd picked from a neighbor's yard, and when she finally placed it on his chest, he fell right to sleep.

He awoke in the desert as a jet flew over, its trail red in the late afternoon. When he rose, he could see Nora, sitting on a far boulder, watching the plane. The sight suggested to him a pleasing pattern, and he imagined that from her spot she saw Roy—his poor, deluded brother—at his own site, tracing the plane's path in the sky.

But then Roy climbed up the rock where Nora was perched. She turned, he spoke, and they climbed down together, out of Green's sight.

Green paused to examine the sudden sour feeling that presented in his heart. What had he seen? What came next?

He listened for a whistle blast. When it didn't come, his fished his gaiters out of his pack and snapped them around his shins. He pulled on a thick wool shirt. He decided to circle around Nora's spot and approach from the wash. Advancing across the flats, he halted occasionally, crouching behind a boulder, dropping into a pan in the sand. The sun was fading, but even in the weaker light objects retained their definition. In the wash he saw the trail of a single desert tortoise, and he followed the trail for a while, crawling alongside until it veered from the direction of Nora's camp. He kept crawling. His skin fit tightly on his face.

"I had this big realization about justice," he heard Nora say as he drew near, unseen. "Now it's gone. But it was super clear for a while." Green slid forward in the sand until he could see her and Roy in the hollow. A slight incline protected him from their view.

"Justice." Roy looked red and sticky. "Strange."

Green's prone position made his bones ache. A theory: people are no more than skeletons, who can, for a short time, walk around.

Nora was arranging rocks into three piles at her feet. "Hmm," she said and then stopped. She reached for Roy and patted his knee. "Are you feeling any better?"

"Yeah. I'm sorry I came over freaked out. I was studying tiny flowers in the sand and looked up at the mountains too quickly." Roy smiled bravely, plucky as an orphan. His eyes went soft, and he appeared to be listening to some faraway call.

"Can I lie on top of you?" he asked suddenly. "It's not sexual."

Nora frowned. "What is it?"

"I promise," Roy said.

Nora studied him for a minute, then pulled her hair over one shoulder and stretched out on the desert floor.

She truly loved Roy, Green reminded himself, motionless, and he had appreciated it, the way she took to his family as if it were her own. He watched as Roy settled himself on top of Nora. She turned her face aside.

"Let's make a deal," Roy said. His voice cracked. "Let's swap souls."

"Leave me out of it," said Nora.

Roy shifted his weight and stared down at her, puzzled. "Do you want me to move?" he asked. "Is this cool?"

"I don't know what this is about."

Roy paused a moment and then rolled off her. Nora stayed where she was.

"All is well," he said.

"Are you asking?" Nora said. "Because I think it is."

Roy stood abruptly. Then he walked fast, away from the hollow, passing not too far from Green's hiding place.

"Roy?" Nora called after him.

Green crawled back down to the wash. A sense of urgency grew like a fungus within him. He could confront Nora and observe her reaction. He could return to his camp and wait out the trip. He rose and brushed off his knees, floury with sand. He could hide all night to see if his brother returned. But there would be other nights. There would always be other nights. He climbed out of the wash to find Roy.

His brother had started across the flats toward Queen Mountain. Green tracked him at a distance. The sun set, and he passed through pockets of warm and cool air. Chollas glowed white in the dusk.

At the mountain's base, Roy picked out a path that rose up the left flank. He wore a head lamp that lit the ground ahead. Green fell in far behind, boots slipping some in the scree. He was mystified by Roy's speed and he began to study his brother's gait. Roy kept his braced leg straight and used his other leg as leverage, lifting from the hip. When there was a large boulder he'd step to it, then take hold of the brace, adjust his leg, and raise it onto the rock. Green tried it. After several paces he tapped into the feel of it, how with each step his brother threw his body off balance, and in the next step, brought it all back.

Then Green tripped and came down hard on his ankle. When he tried to stand, his ankle trembled and wouldn't support any weight.

Roy moved steadily up the mountain. Green watched him, and felt a word form in his throat. But he left it unsaid. Roy climbed on.

Green dragged himself off the trail. He brought his knees to his chest. The important thing was to keep up his body heat, and he knew it was easier to stay warm than to get warm. He made fists and swung his arms in the air. And then he saw it. His father had died. He found out for sure two days later, when his mother collected them on the loop road. But he knew it that night on the mountain. If you let them, visions come to you. You can bring them to your face, like your own hands. Arms lifted, he saw his pale father. When he let them fall, his father disappeared.

Green sat and watched the moon rise from behind Queen Mountain, slow and purple, a flower burning as it bloomed.

At night, the wind sounded like fire. At dawn, the sound was more like a river, moving slowly toward some long-off sea. Green opened his eyes and came back to himself. He was zipped into a sleeping bag. His ankle pulsed. His mouth was dry. There was a bottle beside him, and he freed his arm to lift it, but the water had frozen inside.

"I was on the summit waiting for you," he heard his brother say.

Green sat up. He was on the mountain. Roy bent over the lit camp stove, spooning instant coffee into mugs. Green stayed in the bag and pulled himself near.

"By the time I climbed down, you'd already passed out. I brought up our packs." Roy tapped Green's ankle lightly with the spoon. "You hurt it bad, I think."

Green accepted a coffee and let it steam his face.

"I was waiting for you," Roy said.

Green took a sip and studied his brother. The sun was barely up, but Roy already wore shorts. He balanced on a rock, mug in hand, braced leg straight, with an expression that was almost serene.

"I think I was planning to kill you," Green said.

Roy nodded. "The desert," he said. "It can overwhelm you. Your emotions blow up to match."

"You think it was the desert's fault?" Green said.

"I forgive you," Roy said. "I've felt the same way out here."

"You forgive me?"

"There's a difference," Roy said, "between thinking a thing and doing it."

Birds began. Green drank his coffee and watched the sun go higher and turn the clouds above red.

"Everything blushes upon first touch," said Roy.

Green glanced at him sharply. They had shared a bed for a while as kids, until Green got the idea that with their heads so close Roy could read his mind. Knowing it, each night he'd been flooded with grotesque thoughts he was sure his brother could detect. Then he began to wonder if his brother was actually projecting the thoughts into his brain. Before long he doubted his daytime mind too, scared that not everything in it was his.

Now Green shook his head, trying to recapture what he saw the night before. He set the mug on a rock, closed his eyes, and raised his arms, but this time he only saw water, flat and bone-still. When he opened his eyes, Roy was staring at him, trouble on his face. Seeing it, Green felt troubled too. They were not where they were supposed to be.

"Roy," he said gently.

"What happened last night?" Roy sounded afraid.

"Why don't you tell me?"

"About what happened to you or what happened to me?"

Green tried again. “Can you talk to me straight for a minute?”

“I can’t. ” His brother gave him half a grin. “I don’t want to say something untrue.”

“Roy—” Green stopped and gazed over the valley. From partway up the mountain, he had views of Pine City and the Wonderland of Rocks. Cathedral City was fifty miles to the west. He searched for Nora—he did—but the color of her sleeping bag must have blended into the desert floor.

“Check it out,” Roy said. He raised his hand to a faint print of the moon that remained in the sky.

“The finger pointing at the moon,” his brother said, “is not the moon.”

The moon is not the moon, Green knew, but he kept it to himself.

SHARKS

Sometimes synchronized swimming seduced Nora with its spectacle, but other days it seemed like a sad effort to make plain girls feel like stars. And what was she doing as their coach? She had no patience, no charisma. Water wasn't a metaphor for anything in her life. Still, there she was, on the wooden bleachers in the high school natatorium, overseeing the Sharks' dress rehearsal. Thirty girls waited on the pool deck in full makeup, hair slicked with gelatin, lips pink as cheap gum. They wore sequined suits in an unkind cut.

Maybe it was the wretched suits or the stiffness of the girls' poses or the way the air was so thick it seemed on the verge of condensing to a thing. Nora didn't know exactly, but something about the scene tempted her to can practice and spare everybody the trouble. Except for one inescapable fact: the show must go on. So she pressed PLAY on the vintage tape recorder beside her, and a frantic remix of "Rock Me Amadeus" blasted weakly from speakers at the rail. On cue, the Sharks jerked through their deck work in a mess of angled arms and languid hip thrusts.

Once they dove in, Nora let her mind go. She was getting good at it. In the months since Green had died, she'd been practicing self-hypnosis and meditation to make her head an empty place. To fill up her evenings she rented fitness videos and arty porn movies and carried out multi-course meals from a diner near her house. Weekends she ventured to downtown bars with other single teachers and a few times, on particularly tense, spotty nights, went home with a man she had insulted all evening and had sex with as much aggression as she could muster. Life continued, propelled by nothing, she'd learned.

The song reached its zenith, a demented baritone chorus—*Amadeus, Amadeus, Amadeus, Amadeus, Amadeus, Amadeus, Amadeus, Amadeus, Amadeus, AMADEUS!*—which the Sharks accompanied with shaky ballet legs. At this, the visualization Nora had been attempting (still water in a silver bowl) dissolved and was replaced by a fuzzy, formless, low-grade burn. The Sharks had been practicing in the pool for a month—after six weeks of land walk-throughs—but the finale still looked like crap. Frustrated, she shifted in her seat, and immediately felt a splinter pierce her thigh. She cursed and rubbed the spot where it had entered. In the past few weeks she'd tweezed out dozens, each deserved—probably—for having negative thoughts about what was, after all, her own team. She was starting to contemplate the steel trap of karma when she heard the football coach call loudly from the pool room's upper door.

"Darling, how long will you girls be?" Coach J was at the top of the bleachers, flitting his lashes at her, plastic whistle in spin around his thumb. Against the white of his polo shirt and pukka shell choker, he appeared yellow, but she guessed that was to be expected. He'd recently returned to school after a transplant. Nora was convinced it was her dead husband's liver now valiantly metabolizing inside him.

"I need to get my boys in the water," Coach J continued, swaying slightly, a spacey look on his face. "Give 'em some isometric action. One force opposing that opposite force."

"Twenty minutes," she said, irritated.

Coach J winked, backing out the door with a lame approximation of the moonwalk. Nora massaged her temples. For as long as she could remember she and Coach J had engaged in an uneasy flirty banter that always left some part of her aching.

In the pool, the Sharks floated in three long rows. Prompted by another string of *Amadeus*es, they drew their knees to their chests, raised left legs, and went into awkward flamingo turns. Nora switched off the music. At this point, so close to Pageant, imprecision was painful to witness. The Sharks sat up in the water and chattered.

"Severa." Nora spoke into a microphone attached to the recorder. "Hop out and have a look."

The Shark who had choreographed the number stroked to the side and lifted herself from the water. To Nora, her long, effortless body felt like some kind of rebuke. Watching the girl climb into the bleachers, she fingered the pinches of fat behind her own knees. Severa's breasts were high and fist-sized, her collarbones like two well-made shelves. Her face was painted with waterproof gunk like the other girls', but not enough to mask the bruising on one of her cheeks. All business, she grabbed the microphone.

"Aqua bitches!" the girl screamed. "Concentrate!"

In response, the Sharks drifted calmly on their backs, sculling, waiting to pick up the routine with a set of staggered oysters.

"You got to yell," Severa explained, after switching on the music and settling on the bench.

"I'm not up to it today," Nora said. "My head hurts."

The girl assumed a sympathetic expression, though with the paint job and the bruised face she seemed the one who deserved pity. "I've got Tylenol 3," she said, fumbling around the bleachers where the girls had left their bags.

"What for?" Nora said.

"Wisdom teeth," Severa responded, still looking.

"Don't you need it?"

"I'm in no pain." Severa recovered a brown plastic bottle from her purse. "You want it or not?"

Nora considered it. The last few nights she'd spent awake and alone, listening to the inner lives of the appliances she lived with, regretting every destructive act of her life.

"Maybe a couple," she said.

"Take many," Severa said, shaking pills onto Nora's palm. "I already tried slinging the extras to the Sharks. But these days it's all about speed."

"Hey," Nora protested. "I am a teacher, you know. Authority figure. City employee."

"Oh, I've caught a whiff," Severa said, recapping the bottle. "You smell like renegade to me."

Strangely pleased, Nora swallowed one tablet dry and deposited the rest in her shorts. Then she remembered to glance at the pool, where the Sharks were mangling the barracudas that ended the routine. She shut off the music and lifted the microphone.

"Are you all stoned?" she yelled. "Or just some of you?" The sound of her raised voice through the speakers surprised her. Severa shot her a thumbs-up. The Sharks waited, egg-beatering grimly.

"Synchronization is what we're after!" Nora cried. "What are we here for if not for that?"

"Aw, do whatcha like!" When Nora turned, Coach J was at the door again, a crush of boys swim-suited and throbbing behind him.

"I thought we agreed on twenty minutes," Nora said, speaking into the microphone.

"A wrinkle in time saves nine," said Coach J. "A tisket, a tasket, my girlfriend's got a basket."

"Drunk asshole," muttered Severa. "Fucking musclehead."

Nora looked to the pool. A chain of Sharks was performing an impromptu dolphin, feet hooked to necks, the leader arching back beneath the water, pulling the other girls so they slipped under, one by one. As the last girl's toes descended, the leader's head and chest broke the surface. It was a beautiful trick and, in it, Nora forgot everything. But then the chain came apart underwater and a girl, one of the freshmen, bobbed up, spitting.

"Clear out," Nora said over the loudspeakers, defeated. "Tomorrow we shine."

The Sharks scrambled onto the deck, tugging at their suits

and scooting for towels, while Coach J pumped his fists and fanned his boys' flames.

"Yep, yep, fellas!" he bellowed. "Forty-two hearts that beat as one!"

The football team rushed down the bleachers toward the water. Nora couldn't help but be thrilled by the violence of their feet against the wood and the mindlessness of their unison response.

"Forty-two hearts as one!" they grunted. "Forty-two hearts as one!"

Outside, running laps on the school track, Nora was dizzy. She felt as if she were moving less deliberately than usual, but with more ease, nudged by a force greater than her will. She ran every day after practice, five miles, fifty minutes. She was already in good health, with low body fat and cholesterol and blood pressure. Low everything. But she ran anyway, for the feeling of her muscles extending and contracting, and the numb sensation in her hands as blood was forced to the tips of her fingers.

Three laps down and halfway through four, she saw Coach J by the fence to the parking lot, studying her.

"Keep the knees up," he advised.

She lifted them high, then stopped. What did he know. She walked across the patch of dying grass at the center of the track to where the coach was standing.

"Don't wear yourself out," he said. Smiling, his face was thinner and his chin more sharp.

"I don't see you out here."

"I get my exercise other ways." He blotted his forehead with his arm. "And I used to be the man. In the Guard I'd have to run around carrying one of my buddies on my back."

"Green was in the Guard," she said. "He'd never shot a gun before in his life, but he practiced and won a sharpshooting contest to get an extra weekend home with me."

"I guess Green was the man too." Coach J patted his belly, a gesture of acknowledgment or possessiveness, she couldn't tell. He'd never met Green, mostly because Nora had never felt comfortable introducing them. At school, Coach J would sneak whiskey into her coffee in the teachers' lounge. She'd let him look down her shirt when she stooped to retrieve a napkin from the floor. She had noticed his weight loss and the feebling of his skin, but before she could demonstrate actual concern Coach J had been hospitalized with a failing liver. While he was in, Green died, and the next day Coach J received his transplant. Nora was sure it came from Green, though the reports from the transplant center provided only general demographic and geographic information. One of Green's corneas in a girl from Quincy. A kidney in a senior citizen from What Cheer.

"Thanks for disrupting my practice," she said. "Gracious of you."

Coach J clapped a hand to his chest. "Forgive me," he said. "I shouldn't have stepped on your buzz. But I was anxious to get those boys busy." He reached around and fiddled with the waistband of his shorts, then brought back a small silver flask. "Peace?" he said, offering it to her.

"No," she said. "I'm exercising."

"You call this exercise?" He stepped back from the fence and kicked it. A rattling shimmy of sound. "This track is so flat you could run forever. You need to inject some elevation into the equation. I have the boys run stairs. You should give it a try."

She approached the fence and rested her forehead against the warm wire. If not for the scent of whiskey wafting off the coach, she might have been able to smell the magnolia trees at the school's west entrance.

"You want to race up those stairs?" she asked.

Coach J screwed the top onto the flask and grinned. "Let's go."

Nora squeezed through the gate and followed him into the school, where the day's greasy odor had collected and pooled inside the door. They stood at the bottom of a staircase that rose to a glass walkway leading to the main wing. Coach J balanced on one leg and bent the other behind him to stretch his quad. He wobbled, and Nora felt a qualm.

"Sure you're ready?" she asked. "It hasn't been very long."

He let his leg drop. "Are you ready?"

"As I'll ever be, I guess."

"Likewise."

"On the count of three," she said.

"Three!" He took the stairs two at a time, and she fell behind immediately, foot slipping on the first step. By the time she reached the top, he was already clopping through the walkway, heels kicking, at *her, her, her.*

In the main wing, most of the lights were off. Right behind him now, she could hear Coach J's breath. She could, if she wanted, swipe the sweat from his neck. Instead, she zeroed in on the flask pressed to his back. A series of images presented itself as she ran: Coach J falling, his heart dying, Green's liver recovered and given to a more worthy recipient, a man whom she would follow and observe and judge and—if necessary—challenge to a race, freeing Green's liver for yet another operation. She glimpsed her future, vigilance in motion. She would need to stay in good shape.

"How you doing?" she said, newly imbued with purpose, however fake.

"I'm winning," Coach J gasped before a quick right, to the third-floor stairs. From somewhere came a roaring—she heard it—and as she took the stairs and passed him, she touched her neck and felt the beat there skip.

Her lead widened. But her chest felt rubberbanded. She turned left, up another short staircase. "Finish line," she panted, pointing to the heavy black door at the top. Then something sudden and mean was around her ankle, and she tripped, sort of catching herself, her shoulder taking most of the fall. Coach J blew by, and a second later opened the door—a blast of air—and by that time she had recovered and followed him out, onto the roof, finished. She pitched forward to the gravelly black slate and rolled over. Turning, she could see past the roof's edge to the Great Lawn, and beyond that the freeway, and further, the weathered blue water tower looming over West Des Moines.

From above, Coach J touched her cheek with the toe of his shoe.

"I wish I were you," he said. "Speedy."

"You cheated," she said. "You grabbed me."

"But I won." He reached behind him for the flask. "Loser want a drink?"

She got to her feet and dug into her pocket. "Winner want a pill?"

Coach J put his face so near her hand she felt the force of his words on her skin. "What you packing?"

"Codeine."

"Add to alcohol, and I might stop breathing. I'm already taking a million pills anyway. No thanks. You got yours, I got mine."

"I want yours," she said.

He gave her the flask, and she tipped it to her mouth. Then she threw a pill on her tongue and tipped the flask again. Why not, she thought. Painless and sleepy, what else was there anymore? Poor thing.

"You can really put it back."

"'He said, admiringly.'"

"Most women don't like the flavor of whiskey. It reminds them of their daddies."

"Most women don't like men for the same reason."

"C'mon now," he said softly. "That's not true."

"Maybe," she said, not sure herself.

"My daddy was a good man. He taught me how to tell if china was fine." Coach J demonstrated. "What you do is hold your thumb behind it, like behind the rim of a china cup. If you can see your thumb through the china, if it's that thin, you got good stuff."

"My dad said that's how you judge people." She hovered her arm behind him. "You want somebody transparent, all surface." She clubbed him, lightly. "Easy to break."

Coach J spun around and grabbed her hand, and before she could stop him, slipped off a ring Green had given her, dull silver set with two large stones like purple warts. He forced the ring onto his pinkie. It made the ring nothing and small.

"I don't think it flatters your finger," she said.

"Whose finger would it look good on? Is there such a finger in the world?"

"Here," she said. He didn't need to mock her jewelry.

"It's coming," he said, lofting the ring.

She caught it and wished she had something heavy to throw back. But she wanted to keep the flask.

"So there's a man and a horse," Coach J mumbled vaguely before wandering off toward a distant chimney.

Nora stayed. It felt as if tiny weights had been introduced into the flesh around her eyes. Not an uncomfortable sensation, really. Instead, it helped her focus. *I am filled with myopic energy. I have been loosed from my moorings.* The sentences came from somewhere else. She took some tablets out of her pocket and crushed them against the mouth of the flask. It wasn't all figured out, but impulses came to her: scare him, make him change. This was her chance, she thought, reckless, raising the flask to her lips and blowing the mouth clean of powder. This was her chance to be Green's rescuer rather than his destroyer, her chance to protect and preserve an artifact of his life.

Coach J reappeared, smoothing his belt through his buckle. Before she could lose her nerve, she held out the flask.

"Here," she said.

He took it and rested it on a metal module behind him. Then he caressed his chest and stared past her to something she didn't see.

"Feel my throat," Nora said, on a whim. It was a test she used to run on people. There were different ways to touch a person's throat: as a mother or doctor might, with the tips of the fingers, or like a lover, palms flat on the sides. Or as Coach J did, straight-armed, one hand tight under her chin, like he wanted to lift her off the ground. When she had first asked Green, all those years ago, he'd tilted her head and fit his neck up against her neck, like he was trying to pass something from his throat to hers.

"How's it feel?" she asked Coach J, almost breathless. "Feels to me like there's something in there."

"You want me to get rid of it?" he said. "I could squeeze until it pops out your mouth."

She was a little ill then, from too much desperation in the near atmosphere. Coach J could sense it too, she thought, because he dropped his arm and stepped back.

"How's the swimming show shaping up?" he asked.

She was grateful to talk about nothing. "With everyone in sync, it's actually pretty cool. But get a couple girls lagging and the whole thing is blown."

After that, they fell silent. Nora nibbled on her lip and wondered if he was going to leave. She decided she'd let him. In preparation, she tried to clear her mind with repetition: *Amadeus, Amadeus, Amadeus.*

Coach J picked up the flask. "So was Green much of a drinker?"

"Worried about damaged goods?"

"I don't know what you're talking about," he said, lowering the flask.

"He had some beers sometimes. On the nights he was out with other women. Part of his ritual."

"Sorry," he said.

"He mostly stayed away from the hard stuff. He was more of a cheater than a drinker."

"Not good."

"Here's worse." Tell him everything. Let his pity absolve her. The words as easy as rain slicking off a sloped roof. "He slept with somebody else the day he died. He came home, reeking of smoke and beer and her, and I let him have it. Then, when he went to the bathroom to brush his teeth, I locked myself in the bedroom."

"Sounds about right."

"I heard his car leave. He went to a bar. When he was walking home later, he passed out and cracked his head on the sidewalk. Next time I saw him was in the hospital, on a ventilator. His skin, I've never seen anything that color. They said his brain was already dead."

Coach J flexed his fingers.

"The last thing I heard him say, at home, when he was rattling the bedroom doorknob? He stopped trying. He said, 'If that's how you want it.'"

"The end," said Coach J. He took a pull from the flask before offering it to her.

"Sometimes it's hard," she said, taking it, "to see other people alive."

"I hear you," Coach J said.

Nora swallowed a shot of whiskey and turned away. The sun dropped slowly, the sky a smeary red-blue in its wake. A quiet evening, except for the sound of the freeway traffic below like a measured exhalation of breath. She wandered to the edge of the roof and, dizzy, surveyed the Great Lawn. A few of the Sharks loitered there, and Nora could see Severa, who, for some reason, was wearing high heels. When the Sharks spotted a group of football players coming out of the front entrance in street clothes, they hit the grass and began log-rolling down the hill. Then some of the football players dropped their bags and started rolling too. One caught up to Severa and maneuvered on top of her and stuck his tongue in her mouth. He wasn't her boyfriend, Nora knew. The sight returned to her a memory of high school, when she had cheated on her boyfriend with a neighbor next door. She remembered planning it, as a thrill. But although her neighbor touched her more tenderly than her boyfriend, she had never felt less special, giving in to a dim space inside.

Or maybe that's only how she remembers it now. Maybe back then she was proud she had done it. Maybe she stopped eating, and her eyes burned every morning, and the stem of an apple told her the future, and days were things to be run through, bleary and headlong and sick . . .

Severa was still kissing the boy. Nora unscrewed the flask and upended it. A snake of whiskey slid out, and it was an effort to not let the flask fall with it.

"No," Coach J moaned.

"You have a second chance," she said, returning the flask.

"You don't get it." He shook the empty container. "I've had my second chance. I'm on my third. Whatever's left is all cream."

"So you want to die?"

"Death doesn't scare me. But pain scares me to death." He actually shivered. "And now you've ripped off my skin."

"That's what I do," she admitted. "I'm good at it."

"Don't be proud of it."

"I'm not," she said. "Believe me." A sweep of wooziness overtook her, and she lowered herself to the gravel, wincing as she sat.

"What hurts?" asked Coach J.

"I got a splinter at practice."

"Let me see."

She couldn't determine how best to arrange herself. Finally she flipped onto her belly and looked back. Coach J pulled a Swiss Army knife from his pocket and removed the tweezers. Carefully, he bent to her thigh.

"Bet no one's been down here with a knife before." There was a series of sweet little squeezes before he was through.

"Let me see it," she said.

"Too tiny. It flew away as soon as it came out."

"Sure," she said. "Sure it did."

He shrugged and slid the tweezers into the knife before setting the knife on the slate. From the lawn, a girl cried, "No way!"

"I can see how it might be tough for you to look at me," Coach J said.

"You're perceptive." Why not let him believe it? And really, was it even a lie?

"Thanks. My wife might not agree with you."

"Ah," she said, pretending she'd forgotten. "Now you're cheating on a wife?"

"Who said anything about cheating?" Her cheeks flushed, but then Coach J smiled and said, "You're perceptive too."

"No," she said. "I'm sleepy."

"Get comfortable."

She turned onto her back. The slate undulated beneath her.

"Close your eyes," he said. "Sleepy."

She did and her head detached itself, spun rapidly, then rejoined her neck. She heard Coach J's joints crack as he knelt. She had to restrain herself from licking her lips.

He guided her hand to his abdomen.

"No," she said, panicked.

"Can you feel it?"

"Please."

"Here," he said, slipping her under his shirt. He pressed her fingers to him. "Here."

She kept her eyes closed and touched the scar, that fierce cord. She tried to move higher, to the slope beneath his ribs, her favorite spot on a man's body, but Coach J held her firm.

"Feel it ticking," he said.

"I don't think it ticks."

"Feel it churning. It's breaking things down."

"What's it look like?" she whispered. It would be good to know.

"Brown. With lobes. Like a little armadillo if you were looking at it in profile. Minus the scales."

"And the nose."

"The snout," he said. "No snout."

Her eyes were shut, but she still sensed the sky losing light. After she had decided to withdraw Green's ventilator, she cornered a doctor. "What if I had been with him?" she asked. The doctor advised her not to second-guess. "What if I had been there when it happened?" she insisted, but the doctor didn't answer, breezing past into the hospital's blue glow.

"I want it back," she said now, crying, tears dripping into her ears. Because she should have kept everything, ugly or not. Don't ever wish anything gone.

Coach J spoke from deep in his throat. "Can't have it."

"Give it back."

"Never." Beneath his shirt, he stroked her trapped hand.

With the free one, she prodded the slate for the pocketknife. When she found it, she pressured the knife against her leg, prying out the largest blade. She blinked open her eyes. What else could she lose?

"Give it back!" she bawled. She dug her nails into Coach J's skin and slashed with the knife. The tip caught his shirt and ripped it, loosing a flap of fabric and revealing his tight brown scar and a few fresh dots of blood.

Coach J grabbed the knife and sent it scuttling across the roof. Then he slapped her, hard. Her head rocked, but there wasn't any pain. Maybe he would hit her again.

"I changed my mind," she said. Her tongue was fat in her mouth. "I'm going to kill you."

"Not if I do it first." He leaned in, exhaling a sour mist. "Please," he begged, inches away, "can't you let me do it first?"

This close, she could see the grain of his incoming beard and the dark pores of his nose. A stray lash floated in his eyeball's muck. She thought: *How beautiful a form we have. A miracle, this life.*

"Look up," she whispered, and when he did, pupils rolling, she pressed her thumb to the firm white of his eye. It resisted as much as a grape might, which is to say, hardly at all.

YOUR BIG SISTER

You duck into the alley. The restaurant closed an hour ago, but your big sister's still there, next to the padlocked grease dumpster, dressed in her server's uniform, a cigarette stub shaking in her hand. You'd be anxious too, but you took some stuff, so now you're all set.

"I'm all set," you say, before she loses her nerve. "I've got a barrel and a ladle and a hose."

"So now you're a grease thief," she says.

"Don't say grease," you correct her. "Say, *liquid gold.*"

"Gold?" she scoffs, in the exact way she's always done. "Are you serious?"

"The biodiesel people pay $40 a unit. That's $500 for a few minutes work." The paper mask over your face crackles when you talk.

"A life fueled by garbage," your big sister declares, and for a second you don't know if she means your life or her own. Then she jabs her dead cigarette. "You know exactly what I mean."

"Garbage is money," you say. "Now let's go." The stuff's kicking in and you can sense the cloud on its way.

"*Time* is money, ya dumb motherfucker," and that's when you realize your big sister's bombed. Not surprising—you know the bartender's in love with her and sneaks her special cocktails all shift, a brew of bourbon, bitters, champagne. The chef has a crush on her too, which is how she wound up with a full set of keys to the place.

"Don't say *dumb motherfucker,*" you tell her. "Say, *poor little baby.*"

It's weird, but somehow your big sister's expression goes harder and softer all at once.

"I'm doing this because I want to help you," she says, "but maybe the best help is no help at all."

A jolt of worry. You told your big sister you need one last score to pay off your dealer. You told her this is the final corner to turn and then you'll quit and go back to school. But the truth is there are no corners, you're not going anywhere, you're circling the drain. Is it possible your big sister sees through you?

Just in case, you pour it on thick. "It's like all these waves are coming at me," you say, "and it's only a matter of time before I drown."

Your big sister blinks, but she doesn't cry. She never does. "Let's get this over with," she says.

There's a surveillance camera running, mounted high in the alley, so your big sister has come up with the show you'll put on now: you're a masked, stone-cold criminal who pulls a knife on her as she smokes her post-shift cigarette, then grabs her keys, drains the dumpster, and splits. You get your money, she gets to play victim. It's the perfect plan, except for one problem. You realize you forgot the knife.

"I forgot the knife," you confess.

Oh, the look on your big sister's face. She throws down the stub. "You got to have a weapon. Even that crappy camera can pick up on the fact that otherwise I'd kick your skinny ass."

"I do have the ladle," you remind her.

"Fuck the ladle," she snaps. "You're going to have to hit me."

By this point, you feel like you're showering in honey. "I don't want to hit you," you manage to say, but even before the words pass your lips, you're glancing around for a club.

"No way," your big sister says, catching you. "The least you can do is use your own fist."

The night is passing. Down the street, you hear someone yell, "Surprise!" You and your big sister know either one of you could walk out of the alley right this minute. Knowing this, you both wait.

Then, at your side, your fingers curl.

"Knock me flat," your big sister urges. "Make it look real."

"I'm sorry," you say.

Your big sister sighs. "This is it."

It's crazy how fast your big sister drops when you punch her. You kneel over her, afraid of what you'll see. There's a mark on her face where you hit her, but she seems to be breathing OK.

"I love you," your big sister whispers. "Why?"

And you love her too, more than anything. Or more than almost anything. Because here you are rifling through your big sister's purse for the key ring, here you're popping the lock on the dumpster, here you're flipping the lid. You raise the grate and lean over to check the fluid level. Take a moment to inhale that sweet, heady smell. Lift your mask. Shut your eyes.

Behind you, your big sister mumbles, "I want to go to camp," from what sounds like a million miles away. "Remember the canoes?"

Eyes closed, it's easy to go back there, paddling with your big sister and the rest of the kids on the Des Moines River, late sun slicing the water and her braided hair. Near the dam, you drag your canoes up the bank and sprawl on your sleeping bags to wait for the stars. You lie next to your big sister, and, above you, a leader fires up the mosquito fogger, the dull buzz of its motor a lullaby. Spray drifts and blurs your big sister's face, then settles, slick, on your lips.

Your big sister says, "This is the life."

HOUSE OF TROUBLES

Green stepped out to the porch and the night made it clear to him: somebody was going to die. Snow fell like fists, heavy and sure. His face ached in the wind. Last winter, his brother, an alcoholic, had lost most of his arm in a blizzard like this one, and sometimes when Green was drunk—which he hoped to be soon—he tried to re-create the evening, imagining how Roy's world reversed, so that what was cold seemed as warm as a womb. Wandering home after last call, Roy had plunged one arm into a snow bank before passing out. His wife phoned Green hours later, frantic, and Green found him, but by then the arm was too far gone to save. In the wake of it, something had given up in Green, and now he was reckless, foregoing caution and vows. He had learned. The world waits, always ready to surprise.

His car started on the third try, and he drove the quiet freeway to downtown. Several cars had already skidded off the road, overturning, and rested wheels up like cats waiting to be scratched. He took the Grand Avenue exit and trolled slowly into downtown, looking for a bar that was open, any one. He'd spent the afternoon in a West Des Moines motel with a girl who, like him, was working weekends at UPS for the holiday rush. Back home, his wife Nora had thrown her arms around his neck and then balked when she caught the odor of transgression that pumped out from his heart and through the pores of his skin. She had locked herself in the bedroom. He had left the house.

The Callanan Lounge was open. FLURRIES MY ASS, read its lit marquee. Inside, the only female was the bartender. Her hair was twisted up and held by a pencil, and as she wiped the bar in front of him, he noticed her fingernails, beautiful and clear.

"In honor of the blizzard we got a special on Mai Tais," she told him. "Piña Coladas are cheap too."

But before he could decide, the outside door opened, and he turned to see a pale stalk of a woman stumble in. "Where?" she said, her voice barely there, and then she collapsed as if she'd been too violently blessed.

Green rushed to her. "Should I call 911?" the bartender asked. He lifted the woman and was shot through with pain. That day he had worked hard, moving heavy boxes, so he and the UPS girl could clear out quick.

"No," the woman said and put her feet down. He let her go and she wobbled onto a stool and slumped forward.

"Are you going to make it?" he asked. The bartender drew a glass of water and dropped in ice.

The woman nodded. "It's a cold night," she said. "Poor me has less blood in my veins." She pulled some bills from her jeans, laid a twenty on the bar, and ordered a shot of Cuervo and a Bud Light. Green helped her take off her coat. On her turtleneck was a red heart-shaped sticker that read, BE NICE TO ME—I JUST GAVE BLOOD.

"Be nice to me," she said, catching him.

"All right," he said. He lit a cigarette and ordered a beer. He felt strange, not good, dehydrated or something. His throat was tight.

"I'm Cassie," she said. He raised his glass.

"I took the bus in this afternoon," she said. "I went to the blood center and then afterwards I fainted. They made me stay a while, drinking juice, and then on TV they announced bus service was canceled on account of the weather. The blood people called me a cab, but the dispatcher said it would be a couple of hours before anyone was free. I called my boyfriend, Lee, and he doesn't have a car, so he's got to wait until his cousin gets home from work at midnight. I'm supposed to stay here."

She downed the tequila. The bartender poured her another shot.

"I sell all the time, at lots of places. That's why I fainted. I don't think I waited long enough in between. But Lee, he's out of work and he's not allowed to give blood. He's been in Africa. This was before me."

Green watched her face as she spoke. Her nose was a tulip above that little mouth.

"You're thinking he didn't go. My girlfriend thinks the same thing. She tells me he says it so I have to sell, not him. Honestly, I don't care one way or the other. He's got a tattoo on his cheek that looks kind of African. He describes the place like he's been there. So good it's like I've been there too."

"That's a real gift," Green said. He said it reflexively, but hearing the words aloud, they seemed true.

"Where have you been?" Cassie asked.

Normally he played it evasive in bars. The less they knew about him the more likely they'd believe he was someone else. But tonight he felt too terrible to be tricky, and anyway he was supposed to be nice.

"I've been to Cathedral City," he said, "in southern California. My parents used to take us sometimes as kids, and then they retired there. They opened a shirt shop. My father led desert walks."

"Tell me about the desert," Cassie said.

"Tell," the bartender echoed.

"Sandy," he said. "Quiet."

"We could get that from a postcard," the bartender said. She was drinking a ruddy Mai Tai out of a glass measuring cup.

He shrugged. "Postcards don't lie."

"I'm from Hawaii," the bartender said to Cassie. "They have flowers there as big as your head." She leaned into Cassie's hair. "But they don't smell near as sweet."

The women smiled at each other and whatever passed between them allowed Green a quick image of the UPS girl on the soft motel bed. She liked to lie face down while he touched her lightly, just the pads of his fingers, the sides of his hands. Then she liked him to claw her until bumps rose on her skin.

"What's your name?" Cassie asked the bartender.

"Kelly."

"Oh," she said, "I thought it was going to be Peleula or something."

"I'm not native," Kelly said. "My dad was in the Navy. We lived in Seattle and Denver and New Jersey. Hawaii was my favorite. Hawaii's my favorite place in the world."

Cassie took a swig of beer. "Lee's favorite place is this beach in Africa," she said, putting the bottle on the bar, "where every day you eat yams and peanuts, and you shower in these stalls fenced around with bamboo, and it's so hot you start sweating again as soon as the water stops, and you can't stand to wear underwear, and you nap in hammocks and have bonfires at night, and the sky is black and the stars look so big and close you have to bury your hands in the sand or else there you are, out on the beach, arms in the air, jumping like a fool trying to touch them."

"Wow," Kelly said.

Meanwhile, Green was not well. There was a taste in his mouth that hadn't been there before, and as much as he tried, he couldn't breathe deep enough. But the conversation would not pass him by.

"When are you going to go there?" he asked. "It sounds great."

"Never," Cassie said. "Lee's never leaving Des Moines again. His mom gave him a house when she died."

"But you could go," he said. "Alone or something."

"I love him," she said, in the flat way people do. "It's like we're two halves of a fruit."

She was so young. "There's more to life," he explained. "And more fish in the sea."

"There are more seas," Kelly said, "for that matter."

"Not many," Cassie said. "And if you luck out and find a fish? Why would you walk away?"

"I guess you wouldn't," Green said. He knew you did something different. You crawled away, slowly, with sly looks back. His brother's wife had left Roy, reluctantly, two months after he lost the arm. "I don't think he cares it's gone," she confided to Green on the phone. "I think he wants to disappear, piece by piece." Green replied, "He does want to disappear," and she said she knew that, hadn't she just said so, and then she had hung up the phone.

"I try not to spend too much time in bars," Cassie continued. "No offense to you guys. But they make you think you're missing out on something. You start to think you deserve something more."

"Maybe I do," Green said. "Maybe everybody does."

"Nah," Cassie said. "No way. The fact that you said it means you don't." She finished her beer and picked at the label. "Don't feel bad, though. I don't either."

"Sure you do," he said, though she obviously didn't.

"You don't even know me." Cassie reached for some pretzels nesting in a bowl.

With some difficulty, Green swallowed. "So a skeleton walks into a bar," he said at last, "and goes, 'Give me a beer and a mop.'"

"He's making jokes," Kelly said. "Listen. You're scaring him."

"Next he'll challenge someone to arm wrestle," said Cassie.

"Hey," he said, "be nice to me." He tried to say it playfully, but his voice wavered a little. The women looked at each other, and he saw he was missing out on something. It was no illusion. He deserved something more.

"Why don't I drive you home," he said to Cassie.

"Lee's coming," she said. "I'm supposed to wait."

"Remember her fish," Kelly said.

He ignored her. Easy to do. "Why don't you call him and tell him you found a ride."

Cassie stuck her finger in the neck of her beer bottle and lifted it off the bar. "I guess I could call him and see how long he's going to be."

"Go on," he said. "Do that."

She stood and made her unsteady way to the phone on the wall. He watched her dial, and it wasn't until she started to speak that he turned to see the bartender's angry face.

"Here," she said, grabbing his hand, "let's see why you do it." She tapped the well of his palm. "You have an island on your life line. Your energy's divided. You can't keep your mind on one thing."

"Tell me something good," he said, "or tell me nothing at all."

"Saint Andrew's Cross," Kelly said. "Here between life and fate. You'll save a life. You have the potential to, at least. Have you already done something like that?"

"No," he said. He had been drinking with his brother that night last winter and let him walk home alone. Later, when Roy got out of the hospital, Green had asked him why he'd stuck his arm in the snow. "I was going after something," his brother said. "I thought something was in there if I dug deep enough." "Did you get it?" Green asked. Roy looked at where his arm used to be. "I'm pretty sure it got me," he'd said.

"No," Green said again. "No."

Cassie returned, face flushed, alive. "Lee's cousin's car won't start," she said. "They have a call in for a jump, but the station's running late."

He looked at her, waiting. She smiled, giving nothing up.

"I'm going to call my wife," he said, hoping to shake her, but she was distracted, Kelly already tracing a path on her palm.

At the phone he changed his mind and dialed Roy's number.

"House of Troubles Far and Near!" answered a girl's splendid voice.

"Is Roy there?" he asked.

"Roy, hmm, Roy, well, no, I think not."

"Can you tell him his brother called?"

"I could if the case were not that Roy doesn't have a brother. Roy is what we humans call alone in the world. Not even a right arm with which to talk turkey."

"Listen. Tell him Green called."

"That is alone, mister. Not with no body or thing. Have you a right arm?"

"It's Green. His brother."

"Have you a right arm?"

He sighed. "I have a right arm."

"Make use of it. Don't lament your lot. Not you, sir. You possess more than Roy, God bless him, God save his sweet soul."

Green hung up. Last weekend he had come home late after a bout with the UPS girl and found Nora and his brother in the living room—Roy asleep, head in Nora's lap, her hand on his shoulder, under the sleeve of his shirt. "He wants money to put gas in his car," she whispered, "so he can leave the heater running all night, so he can sleep in it."

"I don't get my check until next week," Roy said, full-voiced, without opening his eyes.

"What's wrong with your house?" Green said.

"I let somebody move in." Roy sat up. "Tonight I do not want to deal."

"Come on," Nora said, "stay here. You can sleep in between Green and me in the bed."

"Ha," Roy said, "ha ha," and Green hoped he'd stop there, but he didn't. "Honey, there's so many people between you and him I couldn't fit." If nothing else, Roy had vision, and Nora knew it. After he left, cash in hand, she turned to Green, crying, and told him he would regret it. "Someday you'll hurt more than me," she had said. He had consoled her, all the while suspecting he already did.

Back at the bar, Kelly still studied Cassie's palm.

"I'm going to give you a ride," Green said.

Cassie gazed at him. Kelly dropped her hand.

"Let's go," Green said, finally sure of something. "I'm taking you home."

Snow had drifted into impossible mountains. Green started the car and chewed on his tongue to distract himself from the cold.

Cassie squeezed her arms. "I need to hear about the desert now," she said, shivering.

"When we were little," he said, pulling into the street, "my brother and I played in the desert all the time. Then one day, he got away from me somehow, he got lost. My dad found him, finally, but by that time he was sunburnt and his lips had swollen up. From then on, whenever we went into the desert I had to tie him to me, with a piece of rope from my belt to his."

The wind outside was a warning. But he paid it no mind.

"I got tired of it, always feeling this pull behind me, so one morning I tie him with an extra-long piece of rope. It's so long I don't even notice when he unties his end. I keep walking for half an hour, until the loose rope snags a creosote bush and jerks me. Then I see my brother's gone."

"Where was he?"

He glanced at her and then he was back in the desert, staring at the dusty rope on the ground. The great quiet all around him. The indifference of the sun. Standing there, he had a moment in which he imagined he'd run fast and hard enough to pull free from his stake. He'd made it! Then it all changed, and he saw himself as the lost one, withering away in the desert while his family went on. Afraid, he screamed for his brother, again and again, until Roy appeared, grinning, from behind a rise of sand.

"Wake up!" Cassie yelled. She pushed him, hard, and the wheel spun through his gloves, sending the car past the shoulder in a direction so inevitable he didn't bother trying to steer. *Take me. Take me.* The car came to rest in a shallow ditch. When he tried to reverse, the wheels spun, and when he took his foot off the gas, the car went deeper.

Cassie opened her door and climbed up to the road. He followed her, stumbling once.

"I can make it from here," Cassie said, hugging herself. "I'm close. You could call for a tow." She pointed to a convenience store on the corner.

"I'm sorry," he said. "Let me walk you."

Cassie studied her feet. She wore cheap thin-soled canvas shoes, already soaked.

"Please," he said. He thought a more humble him might convince her, so he lowered himself to a squat. "I'll be careful." Knees sore, he leaned on a mound of snow that had been plowed over the curb. It was solid against him. He considered the scene. Why not? He bit the index finger of his glove and pulled his hand free. He pawed at the snow, to see what was there.

"Get up," Cassie said. "Don't be stupid. You're going to freeze your skin."

He stopped. That's all it took. He put on his glove and stood.

"Let's go," Cassie said. Still clutching herself, she took a step, but her knees buckled.

"Here," Green said, making a cradle with his arms. "I don't want you to fall."

She circled his neck and he lifted, and then he was sick, ribs tight.

"Can you do it?" Cassie asked.

"Yeah." He staggered forward. Nora had gone through a phase, right after they married, in which she liked him to carry her around the house. "Your job is to keep my feet off the ground," she'd tell him. "You're my burden," he'd say, and Nora would laugh, "You've always wanted a burden like me."

It had been true. Maybe it was still. A burden makes life simpler. You bear it. You bear it, that's all. It hurts at first, like your body's on fire. But keep going, and in time, your burden feels lighter. Until one day, your burden is no longer a burden. It's nothing. It's the thing that made you strong.

"I can do it," Green said.

"We're almost there," Cassie urged.

Up ahead, a man sat wrapped in blankets on a porch swing.

A portable grill flamed in front of him. Green smelled beef. The man leaned over the grill, and the light of it revealed a dark cross stamped on his cheek. When the man saw Cassie in Green's arms, he stood and spit. "Not again," he said. "Son of a bitch."

Green mounted the steps and Cassie slipped from him. "Thank you kindly," she said. Then the man struck Green full in the face. And as Green sank, he realized that for once it wasn't guilt or fear exploding in his chest like a flower. It was promise. One last time.

THREE DAYS DIRTY

KICKS

High-heeled kicks were all wrong for the journey to the rocky beach they called the Lost Planet. Severa hung onto Doug's arm to not fall. Not that his shoes were better. The canvas yawned away from the soles, laces missing. But they stuck to his feet. Magic Chucks.

Kids staggered into the Planet, wide-eyed and thankful, like victims who lived. Jolly B drove in and parked his truck by the lime pit. He played rap on his stereo and dished beers from a bag. A fire burned most nights, puny, with twigs.

One night, fall newly arrived, heat gone for good, Severa sprawled on her back by the fire, criss-crossing her high heels in the air. She was flexible and strong. She was on the synchronized swim team at school.

"Fuck me!" Severa yelled to the glorious night. Most people laughed. Most people were into her then.

Jolly B said, "You should be a stripper."

"You bet," she said, flattered. "I like to exhibit."

"Sick," Jill said. "That's a total step back."

"Shut it," Severa warned.

"We don't need no preachers here," Jolly B said. "We don't need Jill's morals." Severa smiled at him and his white baby teeth.

"Morals exist," Jill said. "Not mine. Everbody's."

"Traitor," Severa said.

Jolly B sneered too. "Tiny-minded twat."

Jill performed a delicate wet cough that suited her. "Go to hell, both," she said. "Plus Severa wouldn't do it anyway. Deep down it makes her skin crawl."

Severa struggled to stand. Her knees cracked, a sound rich inside her. Her toes, stinging, awoke. She stood and, with two fingers, rescued a dead leaf trapped in Jill's hair. When Jill looked up, Severa spit in her face.

"I wouldn't do it," Severa said. "But not for why you'd think. I wouldn't do it because I'm not sure they'd hire me. I'm scared they would think I'm too fat."

Most people were quick to reassure her: Jolly B and Lunar, Steve too, and Dirt, and even Leonard the Fifth. The adoration felt right and she glowed in it, what she had wanted since the start.

Then she spied Doug, silent, moving to Jill, to clean her face with the hem of his shirt. Severa had given him the shirt on his b-day, wrapped up in newspaper and floss. She eyed Doug now and felt, no kidding, like a little kid just kicked by her dad.

Back at the house she started whaling on Doug. She slapped his face, rammed her fist in his gut. He stood, silent, no payback. If he even poked her she'd call his P.O., who'd return Doug to jail right away. She beat on him until her impulse reversed itself, then ran to the front door and put her fist through the glass.

Doug drove her to Des Moines General. She made him take off his shirt to wrap around her wrist. Blood soaked through like an inevitable ink. He stared at the road, and she stared at the strings of his neck. He was skinny, how she liked, with visible bones. She touched his clavicle with the tip of her tongue.

The emergency room was colorless and full of free chairs. They—someone, somewhere—called her name, and a small-fingered lady doctor came to tweeze window from her arm. The doctor stitched her skin tight and wrapped it in cloth. Doug held Severa's intact hand.

"Funny thing is," the doctor said, "the trauma comes not from punching, but from withdrawing your arm back through the glass."

"I should have stayed there forever," said Severa.

The doctor pointed at Doug. "Should have had him break out the window around you."

"Write that down," Severa commanded. Dizzy, so dizzy, yellow and cerulean sparks. "For the future."

"There is no future," Doug intoned. And she took it as more of the generic doom settling upon them like dirt on a wooden box. But the next morning, in an early white hour, Doug and his Magic Chucks slammed out the injured front door. Out and away from her. She paid, she realized when she woke up alone. She paid. She always did pay.

Standard response: cut her hair. One-handed, with her healthy whole hand. Should have gone to a professional, but the thrill of cutting something pain-free! Now reborn as a little pixie, clean-cut, face round and aglow. Afterwards the floor strewn with hair wisps, shed tails of a thousand freak things.

Then a knock on the poor door. It was Jolly B, Doug's best friend.

"What luck," she almost said. "I want to mess with you to drive Doug mad." But behind him she saw Jen, his girlfriend. Bitter, big-titted shrew.

"So I apologize already," Jolly B said. "I don't want to alienate you by questioning. But here goes: is this yours?" From his fingers hung an all-lace black bra.

"Ouch," Severa said, cupping her chest. "I'm only cotton or silk. My nips don't like the rough stuff."

Jen growled. Severa considering biting her before Jen struck first.

"Jen found it in my truck," Jolly B explained. "She thought it was yours."

"Gotta trust your guy!" Severa said, bright, hyper. "Or he'll fall into another chick's arms!"

"Watch it," Jen said. "Let's go, Jolly." He followed her, meek, down the walk.

"Chew off your arm, B!" Severa called after him. "Get free!" She closed the door and slid to the carpet. A few nights earlier she and Doug had been loop-scooping downtown with Jolly. The guys rode in front where the music was loud. She had the open cab all alone. Bored, she teased some farm boys cruising behind them. She worked her arms out of their sleeves and removed her bra. She wrapped the bra around her neck, pretended to hang herself. The farm boys mooned her. She lapped at the night air. The farm boys sped up to Jolly's bumper and honked. "Cow-fuckers!" Jolly B screamed, and Doug, silent, stuck his knife out the window. The farm boys fell back and took the next turn. She had pushed her bra under Jolly B's spare tire then, a strap peeking out, shy and black. Because playing with people was fun. That was something she knew.

Severa took a cigarette from a pack on the table and went to the stove to light up. She had left her bangs long, and when she leaned into the burner, her hair curled up and caught fire. She smelled it, sharp and scary, something not supposed to be burnt. She dropped the cigarette and slapped at her forehead. The impact made her teeth hurt. Then she broke off crisp bits of her hair, as easy and nothing as an old person's bone.

She found Doug's stash zipped into their mattress. The danger revealed itself after two bowls of his pot. He would have somebody mess her up. She'd ruined his shirt, left a mark on his face. He had friends. She had the opposite. Her hand pulsed, agreeing. Oxygen escaped through the hole in the door. Rope, baseball bats, sirens. Cruel Doug, leaving her alone, half-sunk in terrible vision.

The pages in the phone book were as thin as toilet paper. She flipped through the yellow ones until she found Domestic Abuse. She scanned the short list and picked Victims, Inc.

When someone answered, a steady voice, female and warmer than blood, she cried into the phone, "Help me! Please help!"

The counselor, Christina, explained the cycle of violence. They were in the intake room at the shelter. No windows and an uncarpeted floor. On Christina's small desk was a green plastic plaque.

It read, in block letters, GO PEACE.

"Tension builds," Christina said, "and you feel like you're walking on eggshells, like any minute the ax falls."

"Right," Severa said. "Exactly."

"Then boom! The explosion."

Severa raised her wrapped wrist as evidence.

"And finally, the most insidious, the thing that keeps the circle closed: the honeymoon period. He tries to woo you back. He sends flowers. He says never again."

"You're a dyke, right?" Severa asked.

Christina didn't blink. "That's right."

"Your arms are so worked. That's how I knew."

"Not all of us have strong arms."

"I heard you guys have a spy network, like a pussy patrol. So you always know if your girlfriend is cheating."

"Words travel," Christina said calmly. "I'm sure that's true in your world as well."

"Do you try to convert the women who come here?"

"We don't recruit, if you're asking."

"Be a sister and fist her?"

Christina stood and leaned across the desk until she was so close Severa could smell her tongue. A little something like fresh-brewed sun tea.

"If you don't want the pep talk, just say so," Christina said. "You're a bigot, but I'm here to help anyway. Not even a little oyster like you deserves to be hurt."

"My boyfriend eats them raw," she said, happily. This was better. She hated women who acted like women, hiding their mean. She knew they all wanted what she had. She hated most men too, dull and easy to read. One of her projects, along with learning to knit, was to transcend gender altogether. In fact, she almost had. So close that one night, magic-drunk at the bar on the corner, she had paused in front of the marked restroom doors and wondered, for real, "Which is me?"

Severa sat on her bunk in the sleep room, a green-walled square place with a window stuck up with so many decals it looked like stained glass. She smoked, ashing into the folded-up cuffs of her jeans. She stamped out the cigarette, then reclined on the bunk. Self-truths came to her. The first was that she was a Buddhist. She'd given up grasping. Her hands were open and flat.

Then she stopped thinking and went to the phone in the hall to call Jill.

A vicious machine answered. "This is for Doug," she said after the tone. "Tell him I'm weak, tell him I need someone to do for me." He liked it when she made herself small enough to fit into his wallet. She wanted to say more, but a woman, a shelter resident, appeared at the other end of the hallway. The woman came toward her, fast.

"You called your abuser?" she asked.

"That ain't allowed?" Play dumb, Severa thought. Fracture words.

"Some of us want things to get better."

"If you learn anything here," Severa said, "learn this. Ain't no better to get."

"I have to tell Christina you broke the rules," the woman said ruefully. "I don't want my trouble finding me."

"Look what he did." Severa pointed to the bandages. "He dunked my hand in boiling water."

"And you called him."

"Don't make me go back."

"You're going back," the woman said. "That's what you've chosen."

"In case you haven't heard, I'm disempowered. I don't even have access to choice."

"You have to feel to be able to choose," the woman said. "There has to be something you want."

Severa considered. "I want to be able to breathe underwater."

"That's good."

"I want a day of the week named after me."

"You got it."

"I want to kick the shit out of you."

The woman smiled, a slow one that started in the center of her lips and moved out from there. "Go on," she said finally. "Choose violence, choose shame. Choose bad often enough and one day you'll realize it's not working. You'll choose different."

"Come look at this world." Severa swept the air with her fingers. "Notice that it's disgusting. Dive to the bottom." She took a step closer. "Stay with me. We'll hang out."

"That's right, babe," the woman said in a soft, encouraging voice, one you'd use to coax puke out of a drunk. "Keep on choosing bad. Then when it all falls apart, choose good."

"How about instead I choose you?" Severa said. She made her voice wiggle. "How about you teach me the way?"

The woman stared at her, then put her hands on Severa's shoulders and eased her forward into an embrace. She scratched Severa's back, softly, in diminishing concentric shapes.

Once Severa's dad had slapped her, which shut her up, and then he looked too pleased with himself, and his pupils grew big, and his hands curled to fists, and he stopped breathing, and she yelled out a question, anything to change the direction in which everything was headed: "If you could be anyone, who would it be?" Her dad paused, fist by his ear, and said, "The late, great Janis Joplin." Then he blinked and his cheeks were covered in tears. At that moment, her notions exploded. The world disclosed itself, cross-sectioned and pink. Everyone should be like her dad, she'd realized, steel-shelled, soft and sloppy inside.

"So, so stupid," the woman said kindly, still scratching.

"Get off," Severa said and pulled away. "You're easy as pie."

The night surprised her. She hated to miss the day getting dark, hated when night suddenly appeared, like a flasher in the playground. After expelling her, Christina had driven her to the Hy-Vee, where Severa bought a two-liter bottle of Pepsi and called a cab. The low curb she waited on leached the warmth from her ass. She took a long drink from the bottle. One thing about Doug—he couldn't tell stories or explain away mysteries or play guitar, but he kissed with a perfect restraint that maddened her, that made her want to bite his tongue right out of his mouth.

When the cab arrived, she sat up front with the driver, propping her feet high on the dash. Ash fell from her cuffs to the floor mats. She admired her kicks. Wearing them, her ankles looked frail, her toes like little pale morsels of pork.

"Nice shoes," the cabbie said flatly.

"Are you mean?" she asked him. He had dry hair and too-long front teeth.

"When I got to be," he said. "Sure I am."

"How about Armenian?" she asked. "Are you that?"

"I'm homegrown," he said. "Corn-fed. I'm Iowan. I do people right."

"Do you go to strip clubs? Do you cheat on your girl?"

"I said I do people right. What does that mean?"

"You tell me," she said.

They drove on Fleur, past the flooded mess of Waterworks Park and the abandoned Holiday Inn, decaying.

"How did you mess up your arm?" the cabbie asked.

"My girlfriend," she said. "She's real jealous. She saw me kissing this other girl and she freaked. She slashed at my wrist with a knife."

The cabbie cleared his throat and his nose twitched. "Does it hurt?"

"You know how it is," she said. "It's less painful than being alone."

"I wouldn't know about that."

"Great for you," she said. "You're loved. Aren't you so incredibly it."

"Where you going anyway?" the cabbie asked. She'd told him to head for the airport.

"I'm hopping a flight to Girls Town," she said. "I'm winging my way to Nirvana."

"Look," he said. "I'm too beat for this shit. Tell me where you want to get let off."

She directed him to Blue Lights, a vast high-fenced parking lot across the street from the airport. She gave him $15 and left the Pepsi in the passenger seat. She told him to wait.

Blue Lights was cool-lit and almost vacant, regularly overflown by planes. She and Doug used to go there on long nights, and eat lemonade concentrate out of the can, and dance cha-cha to no music at all. Summer bugs in swarms, biting, trucks rushing by, ashamed of their size. Perfect.

There were a few empty cars. She sprawled on one's hood. She let the night's silence rest on top of her, like a sleepy little kid. Then she heard it: a plane, rising, screechy, fired up. When it passed over, close enough for her to read the numbers on its belly, close enough to feel the engine in the empty places of her skull, she scissored open her legs and yelled, "Fuck me!"

She had told the cabbie to wait. Because all she needed was someone to see her. The rule of the world is so obvious. The only way to get by is to make yourself low. Make everybody feel like they're looking down on you.

She yelled, "Fuck me, fucking fuck!" Her legs ached. The cabbie honked twice before driving off. It's working, she thought. Yes, it is!

GOOD MONKS

Later that night, a delirious moment. Picture this. Pale man shouting, "I am drunk on water and the bitterest love!" In the near-empty diner his voice surprising as a first drop of blood.

Severa eyed the man from her booth along the glass wall of Andy's Eats. She was stretching a cup of coffee into the infinite, sip by sip.

"Water!" the pale man shrieked. "Love!" His table was in the center of the diner. On it, onion rings and a brown malt, untouched. Two streaky-haired kids seated at a long chrome counter spun on their stools and waggled their boots at him. Severa recognized them as sophomores from school. They were only chippers, occasional flyers, not too hardcore.

"Kool-Aid!" one of the kids yelled.

"Insanity!" said the other, cracking up.

A waitress tending to a candy display at the register sighed. Her eyes looked like cranberries. Her arms disappeared into a carton of Zagnuts.

"Water!" the pale man screamed again.

The waitress withdrew from the Zagnuts and started toward him.

Severa adjusted her cross-body bag and walked to the man, arriving before the waitress. Coming right up, mister.

"He's mine," she said, grabbing the man's arm. "I'll take him."

"Yours?" the waitress asked.

"For now and maybe always." She worked her hand up the wide sleeve of the man's coat. He quieted in her hold.

"Why weren't you all at the same table?" the waitress asked. "Why were you letting him scream?"

"You have beautiful eyes," Severa told her.

"So you're going to pay for him? Since he's yours and all?"

Severa tugged on the man until he stood. "I can let him sit here and scream," she said, "or I can get him out of here."

"You can't pay for him?"

"Let's see if he can pay for me." She spoke loudly to the man. "Do you have money? Can you settle your debts?"

The man reached inside his jacket and came back with three perfectly folded bills.

"There. Now we're all square." Severa placed the money on the table. The waitress seemed uncertain, so Severa repeated, "You have beautiful eyes."

The waitress's face dimmed as she worked the question: complimenting or making fun?

"If you weren't on duty," Severa cooed, "I'd ask you home. I have this peppermint lotion I could rub on your feet."

For some reason, that decided it. The lady's whole body went stiff.

"Bitch," the waitress said, "get out now."

Outside, beyond the nimbus of the diner's floodlight, the night was at its darkest, hoarding all. Someone somewhere was playing bad chords on a guitar. Severa bit her lip. Doubt and worry, worry and doubt. In the diner she had made more waves than was good for her.

"I'm drunk on water," the man said, softer now, on the sidewalk. Under his coat his arm was fleshy and bare. Severa gave it a few squeezes.

"Goes down easy, don't it," she said. So all right: she needed money. Doug had left her. Alone, she had nothing. And she needed to eat, didn't she? She did!

"Water," the man said dully. "Oh, water."

"What about bitter love?" she said. "Don't forget that."

The man stumbled forward a few steps, but she didn't let him go. There was a slat bench up against the diner wall, and she led him to it, to get a better view. A slight guy, with smooth skin and single-lidded eyes.

"What's your name?" she asked.

"Somvay," said the man.

"Lola," said Severa.

Somvay slapped his cheeks lightly and drew a deep breath.

She sat next to him. A thick wig, a bandanna stretched over her head like a mantilla, dark glasses, and lots of makeup, but still she nuzzled into Somvay when a car drove past them, casting its white pitiless light. Better safe.

Somvay touched her arm. "What happened?" he asked, motioning to her bandaged wrist.

"I fell," she lied. "I was running after my dog and I tripped. Silly me."

"Where did you get your dog?"

"The shelter," she lied again.

"Good. You saved it from death."

She studied him. "Buddhist?"

"Yes."

"Me too! I have a book in my bag. Later on, we should chant, chant, chant."

A hick girl in tight jeans swung past the bench then, massaging the neck of the boy walking with her.

"Fuck him!" Severa yelled. "I did!"

The girl turned quickly, like she might start something, but then she kept walking. That's right, chick.

In Severa's bag was a roll of duct tape and a thermos of beer with codeine stirred in. The idea came from Doug. He used to go ganking with his ex-girlfriend. The ex-girlfriend would dress tarty and lure a drunk weakling somewhere lonely. Then she'd drug him or Doug would hit him and they'd take everything he had. To Severa, it seemed heavy on effort as compared to reward, but Doug was convinced it was worth it, the chance of getting caught low. When the mark awoke, disoriented and embarrassed, he was unlikely to go to the police. And even if he did, his story would be fuzzy. Doug didn't want to go back to jail.

"I'm drunk," Somvay repeated.

"Why you drinking tonight?"

"The problem is I love women," he said.

"They're the worst." Severa handed him the red thermos from her bag.

"I'm not from here." He unscrewed the cup cap and poured himself a drink. "I feel a little lost."

"I get it." Severa patted his leg. "Des Moines sucks."

Above, the moon peeked out of a neat envelope of clouds. Then the air was heavier and heavier until it started to come down around them as rain.

"Oh no," Somvay said. His shoulders sagged.

"Close your mouth," Severa commanded. "We don't want you more drunk."

The taxi driver was as tanned as a detasseler. Severa put Somvay in the car and settled into the front seat. She figured the driver would look at her less than if she was in back, with him working the rearview mirror.

"So I heard ugly prostitutes let johns get away with more," she told the cabbie, once they were moving. "The rule of the marketplace makes it like that."

"The market is a suffering place," said Somvay from the back.

"Don't mind him," Severa said. "He's a major Buddhist. Me, I appreciate works way more than faith." She drew close to the cabbie's ear. "What good things you done lately?"

"I've done a few."

"Please," she said, "tell me about your good things. At length."

"Well," the cabbie drawled, "there is a certain length I could tell you about."

"I'm drunk," said Somvay.

Severa passed back the thermos.

"About that length," the cabbie said. His voice was easy, but she could hear the meanness underneath. Great.

"How long?" she asked.

"Until what?" Somvay leaned into the space between the front seats.

"Have to say I've never measured," the cabbie said. The moon had moved and now lit the bronze hollows of his face.

"Pain," Somvay broke in, "is what you measure pleasure by."

"No, pumpkin," Severa corrected him, "pain is what you measure pain by."

"Both of y'all are wrong," the cabbie said. "Pleasure is what you measure pleasure by." And then his red fingers were up on her thigh.

Right on. "Stop the cab!" she yelled. The cabbie, unbothered, pulled to the curb. Severa threw open the door and called for Somvay to join her. He did, stepping gingerly out of the car. The rain was almost nothing now.

"You owe me ten bucks, girlie," the cabbie said.

Severa steadied Somvay on the sidewalk, then marched around to the driver's side. Smiling her wicked smile, she bent to his open window. "I owe you shit. You're lucky I'm not reporting you. You'd never drive a cab again."

The cabbie grabbed her head. His hands covered her whole ears. "Listen, honey," he said, pulling her in, fingering the bones of her skull, "I'm giving you this one for free. This lesson. It's easy picking up a bruise. It's real tough getting rid of it."

"Thanks, wise man!" she said, jerking away. She danced to the sidewalk and threw a rock as the cab drove off.

The rock missed. Severa cursed. It was a bad sign.

They made their way through dense woods to the Lost Planet. Not easy—a slick weedy ravine, train tracks, a faint path to the rocky beach. A lime pit at the Planet foamed purple, Des Moines's own terrible sea.

Severa removed her dark glasses and held fast to Somvay by the loops of his jeans. He stepped tentatively with not enough bend in his knees. When they arrived at the bank of the pit, she let go of him for a moment, to squeeze some dampness out of her wig. Somvay tripped and ended up on all fours.

"Come on," she said impatiently, kneeling. "Let's attempt to remain upright."

Somvay raised himself to a squat and tried to brush the mud off his coat. "Where are we going?"

"Don't ask," she said. "That's not the right question."

His face was flushed, so she untied the bandana from her hair and wiped his cheeks. She dried his ears, and his sweat wet her fingers through the cloth. When she was little, her dad had worked summer construction, and when he came home sweaty, he shook salt into his palm to lick off. He said it was to replace what he'd lost during the day, and she loved seeing him do it. It seemed smart. One hot August she ran laps around the block in a wool sweater so she could come in and eat salt straight too, like her dad. Instead she fainted and broke her head on the sidewalk and a neighbor lady drove her to the hospital to get stitches.

"I have to go to work," Somvay said.

"Work?" she said. "It's too late for that."

"I'm graveyard," Somvay said. "At the start of the line. The hogs come by, and it's three fast cuts with the saw."

"You're at the meatpacking plant?"

"The kill floor. It's cold. Like the bottom of a lake. There's blood on my shoes, all the time."

"Are you the one who kills them?"

He shook his head. "They're already dead when they get to me."

"That's better, right?"

"Better than what?" He scratched his cheek, and Severa could see his nailbeds were pink with infection. Three T's were tattooed in a triangle on his thumb.

"Toi O Gica," Somvay said. "It means I don't care about anything."

"For real?"

"I care about everything," Somvay said. "That's why I'm tired."

"Lie down then." She gave him a little shove, and he sat, heavily. "Lie back."

When he did, his shirt rode up, revealing his smooth belly, the aching cut of his hips. He really was beautiful, and for a second she considered changing plans. But instead she set her bag on the ground and straddled him, pushing his arms over his head. She retrieved the roll of tape and taped his wrists together.

"I'm lost," he said.

Severa slid back and pulled his canvas shoes from his feet. No socks, so she applied the duct tape to his bare ankles. She was starting to sweat under her wig so she removed it and put it on the ground.

"Oh," Somvay said. "You plan to kill me."

"What?" She stopped. "Who do you think I am?" She repositioned herself, knees close to his body.

"I work hard," he said, "but for what?"

"Forget work." He wore a delicate silver chain high on his

throat, and when she touched it, she felt his pulse. "Think about play."

"At the wat," he said, "I used to play soccer, and one day when I kicked the ball it hit a monk in the head."

Behind them, the terrible sea gurgled.

"The monk looked at me," he continued. "Then he bowed and said, 'Thank you for the opportunity to practice patience.'" Somvay brought his arms up an inch from the ground and she felt him shift beneath her. "Now I thank you. For reminding me I own nothing. Not even my body."

"Cut it out," she said. Why was he taking this where it wasn't supposed to go?

"Oh, well," he said, "whatever, never mind." He laughed, and it was like a red scarf in the air.

She couldn't help herself. She kissed him on the lips, once, and when she stopped, his eyes were shut, his breath light. She taped his mouth and reached under him for his wallet. Inside a credit card—she could use that tonight at least—and thirty-five dollars cash. Behind the bills was a cracked photo, and when she removed it, she saw a young monk in orange robes, lacquer bowl in hand, standing beneath a well-leafed tree.

She studied the monk and then looked at Somvay. The same high cheeks and soft chin. She slid the photo and credit card into her bag and laid the wallet by her wig. Then she rose and circled Somvay's still body. The terrible sea, the terrible sea. For a second she imagined floating across it, away from her dirty little life, until she hit some different, greener shore.

But everything's working, she reassured herself. I'm alive. Isn't that true?

Then she heard. The growl of an engine, a dark beat pumping through bad speakers. She grabbed her wig and bag and reached under Somvay's arms. He was out. Holding her breath, she dragged him to a spread of brush, dirt funneling into where his jeans gaped from his waist. When she heard the vehicle pop over a log blocking the Planet's secret path, she dropped Somvay and moved away into other weeds.

A truck careened into the Planet. Two men in the cab. And then she saw Somvay's wallet near the bank of the pit. And his bound ankles, not quite in the weeds, shined on by the big moon.

Severa huddled in the dirt. The men were first-class cranksters, she could see right away, scabby and bone-thin. Skinny little zipheads, she told herself. And hadn't her dad once showed her some killer judo moves? But then again, the crank had probably made the men paranoid enough to pack heat.

Still: the wallet. Somvay in the woods. Severa closed her eyes and slowed her breath and tried to tap into the vibes of any good forces that might be lurking, able to help. For a second she felt dizzy, which was promising. But then she remembered it had been a day since her last meal.

No matter. No running away. Not yet.

The men had left the trunk's headlights on, which lit the clearing nice and bright. One of them, a blue-skinned guy with long arms, hurriedly fired a camp stove and unloaded boxes of chemicals and a collection of small empty jars. The other, small and hairless, cut open a series of Vicks inhalers, removed the cottons, and mixed them with water in a glass meatloaf dish.

"I bumped into this girl last night," she heard the bald man say, "this South-of-Grand girl, and she goes, 'Trade you the rings off my fingers for a gram.'"

The blue man sprayed starter fluid into a jar and shook it until there were clouds inside. "I'd have said, 'How 'bout you give me your fingers instead?'"

The bald man frowned.

"Hell, I'd bite off her fingers myself!" the blue man said.

"Nice," said the bald man. He dumped a cupful of clear fluid into the meatloaf dish and balanced it on the camp stove. A smell like nail polish remover made Severa's eyes tear.

Something rustled the high grasses around her, something stronger than wind. When she looked, Somvay was squirming. She slid toward him, keeping an eye on the clearing. In their rush to cook up, the men had missed the wallet and the ankles both, but now Somvay was getting noisy. Kneeling behind him, she pulled his body—slowly, slowly—further into the weeds. His eyes blinked open. A sound burbled in his throat. Could he breathe? Watching the men, Severa held one finger to her lips and untaped his mouth.

"Water," Somvay said.

The blue man looked up.

"Quiet," Severa whispered fiercely. "None here."

"Who's there?" the blue man said. He started toward their hiding weeds, and Severa saw the gun in his pants. So she retaped Somvay's mouth and stepped into the clearing. It was exactly like going onstage.

"Hey, you seen a big guy running around out here?" she said. "I lost track of my giant boyfriend somewhere in these woods."

The men appraised her. She tried to look ugly and old.

"You're not law, right, dressed like that?" the blue man asked.

She made herself giggle stupidly. "No, these are date clothes! My boyfriend and I come down here on weekends and practice with his gun."

"Glad to hear it," the blue man said. "I've been in jail once and I'll kill somebody first before I'd go back."

"You'd kill yourself before going back," the bald man corrected him.

"Is that what I said?" the blue man asked Severa, grinning. "Did my brother hear me right?"

She ignored the question. "You two are brothers?"

"We're brothers," the bald man said. "You can call him Luke and me Pat."

"But we're not like your brother," blue Luke said. "That's one crazy brother, leaving a little girl alone in the woods."

With men, Severa knew, the key is to never let them think they're scaring you. Don't give them anything. Just get away.

"Enjoy your crappy redneck heroin," she said. "I'm gone."

"Wait a minute," Luke said. "I'd hate to chase you."

She stuck in her place.

"If you're lost, it's no good to run all over."

"Better to stay still," advised Pat.

"All right," she said, voice light. "I can hang for a time." She found room for herself between a pile of Prestone cans and a box of Red Devil Lye.

Luke took a step toward her and sent the cans clattering with his foot. Then he settled into the empty space he'd made. His neck was dirty over the collar of his shirt. His pupils were as big as dimes.

Severa stared back, trying to be cool. She had a plan. If he made a move, she'd yell, "Thank you, Lord, for sending him!" If he kept going, she'd whisper, "Praise Jesus for every act you do." That might make him lose his nerve.

In the meantime, she yawned and twisted away from him, pretending to stretch. She cast a quick glance toward where she'd dropped Somvay. Her stomach wobbled when she saw him sitting head above the grass line, arms untaped. He was going to free himself. Then what about her?

Her spine cracked, and she twisted back to center. Pay attention, girl. That's everything now. Her best hope was that these guys fixed and left fast.

"Can I see your gun?" she asked Luke sweetly, to distract him.

He took the gun from his waistband and pointed it at her.

Not so scary. In fact, something about a gun in her face made her feel like she was exactly where she was supposed to be.

"Come on," said Pat. "That's uncool."

"You think?" Luke let the barrel hover eye-level a few seconds more and then stood and replaced the gun in his pants. "All right. Night's long. Besides, I got to go drain myself of poison before I put new poison in."

"I have to piss too," said Pat.

"Why don't you first stay with her," Luke said. "We sure wouldn't anybody to be alone." He loped toward the truck, slow and easy as a cop.

Severa watched to make sure he didn't veer toward Somvay. The she turned back to Pat. He avoided her glance, scrambling up to gather the cans his brother had scattered. His ears were dull yellow and scarred.

"What's with them angry ears?" she asked.

He paused and used a can to poke one lightly. "I was a firefighter," he said. "These days they got helmets with protectors. Back then, your ears were out in the air."

"Poor you," she said, pretending sympathy.

"It was better before," Pat said. "Your ears were antennas. Hot ears meant it was time to bail." He let the cans fall from his arms into a brown Hy-Vee bag. "Fellas today can't feel it. It's too late before they even know."

Severa eyeballed him sharply. Was this iced-up tweaker trying to tell her something? Was he, in fact, a smart guy?

Pat wasn't saying. He wasn't even paying attention to her anymore. He knelt by the camp stove, warming his hands and scanning the black sky. "I loved that job," he said. "I loved my chief like he was my own father. If he pointed me to the Gates of Hell, I'd have grabbed a hose and charged in."

"You know," she said, trying to play his sudden softness, "I think bald guys are the smartest and most soulful of all guys. It's like without hair to worry about they have more time to think deep."

Pat massaged the sweat on his face up to his scalp. "You're putting me on," he said. "Still, I ought to let you run right now. But what Luke would do . . ." He whistled. "Go along nice is all I can say. Don't make things worse than they got to be."

Her blood sped through her, getting her woozy. She took a deep breath and watched the dish on the fire steam. Over the summer she and Doug had tried to make raisins by drying grapes on a blanket in the sun. While they waited, Doug had her do bong hits. Pretty soon she was all over that blanket, popping hot fruit with her teeth.

"My turn," she heard Luke say. Then he was squatting next to her, smelling like a sick cat. His brother got to his feet and jogged toward the truck. Severa prepared to fight.

But Luke had other things in mind. He arranged his works on a rock, took a packet of crystal from his pocket, and fixed a shot. His muscles tensed. A rare color came to his cheeks.

"Sooo," he asked when he was finished, "where do you think your brother is now?"

She was rethinking the whole boyfriend tale. Luke might like the idea of having to use force. Best plan was to get the brothers beating on each other, in the wild of their after-shot flash.

"I'm talking to you," Luke said. He toyed with the hem of her shirt. His finger bled from the tip. When it brushed her leg, her quad flexed against her will.

"Stop," she said. "I don't want your poison blood on me."

"I asked you a question." He moved the finger to her wrapped-up wrist. She already had a story made about spraining it during karate, but Luke didn't ask. He touched her neck, and she cleared her throat and spoke.

"You seen right through me, guy. You know I don't have a boyfriend. I'm playing coy."

"Coy," Luke said softly. Then he kissed her.

"Your mouth is like trash!" she spit, pushing him away.

Luke grinned, eyes strobing. "Anyhow, I'm too speedy to fuck. At present."

She forced a chuckle. "Oh, who I am fooling? I saw something with you and me right away. The thing is, your brother's coming on real strong."

"Yeah?" Luke knuckled his eyebrows. "He always wants what's mine. But I cut him slack again and again. You know how it goes. Next to water, blood's thick."

"Next to water, everything's thick," Severa said. "But there's more you should know. Your brother said we should gank you and snatch the crank and run."

Luke's face darkened. "One night," he started. "One night, my brother died three times. Three! But I kept bringing him around. I sat by the tub and kept him alive." He ground his teeth. "This is how I get paid back?"

"He said you barely got enough brains to keep your body breathing. He said your head's full of meat."

Thank you, crank, for how fast you turn a person upside-down mad! Luke began a scratching and grumbling spree, clawing at his cheeks and the inside of his arms. He kept at it until his brother returned and sat cross-legged, folding his hands nicely in his lap.

"You talk to this girl?" Luke demanded right away.

"Sure I did," said Pat.

"You say anything I should know about?"

"I might have made a suggestion." Pat polished his head, sheepishly, with his sleeve. "But forget her. Let's get to work."

Luke's chest heaved like some tacky romance starlet. His nostrils blew out like a bull in the ring. It worried Severa some. Had she pressed the guy too hard?

"Why don't you turn on the music in the truck first," Luke said. "I'll get you fixed up."

Pat struggled to his feet. "All I do anymore is get up and walk," he complained.

As his brother left, Luke dumped a half-spoon of lye crystals into a bottle, added water, and shook until the pellets dissolved. A dark path appeared in Severa's mind—liquid lye?—but she tried not to take it. She looked past the lime pit to where downtown flickered pink, like it was on fire. When she looked back, Luke was pressing his blue lips together as he drew the lye into a syringe.

Hard Spanish rap boiled out of the truck. Pat jittered back, shaking his fists like maracas. Luke handed him the shot and a length of brown tube.

"Hold on," Severa said, but Luke clapped his hand over her mouth, hard enough to make her cavities ache.

"You're next," Luke told her. Pat tied off. He got ready and pressed the plunger down.

"I feel bad," he said after the needle hit the vein. Then the plunger broke off in his fingers. He pulled the shot away. There was a mark where the needle had pierced the skin. He stabbed at it with the broken syringe.

Luke let go of her and grabbed the shot and threw it into the lime pit.

"Don't!" Pat groaned, white.

Luke wiped new tears from his eyes. "Oh Jesus," he said.

Pat dragged himself closer and touched Luke's shoulder. "It's OK," he said. "Just hurry and fix me one more."

"My own only brother," moaned Luke. "How could I?"

Severa knew the right move now was to bolt, before Luke turned and said, "Look what you made me do." But when she stood to leave, he drew the gun.

"Take it," he ordered. "Shoot me in my brain. If he goes, I'm going too."

"Stop," objected Pat. He stood, then went ghosty and sank to the ground.

Luke spoke only to her. "Shoot me in my brain before I shoot you."

Severa took the gun. Holding it made her hand so much bigger. She was so much bigger. Do you realize how big you can be? Even raising the gun to her temple didn't shrink her. Even the barrel against her ear.

"Not you!" Luke insisted. "Me!"

She'd always imagined a real peace would come right before kicking. She waited for something, touching the trigger, but nothing appeared. It surprised her. Until the instant it happened, did you stay right here?

"Who's that?" Pat said then, before falling into a full faint. Luke let loose with a sob and hunched over his brother in the sand.

Severa turned to see Somvay approaching on bare feet. Silver tape flapped at his ankles. His coat hung wrinkled and loose. The lipstick on his chin from when she'd kissed him now—of course—looked like blood. Still, he seemed calm.

"I probably shouldn't have done all this," she said, lowering the gun.

Somvay's cheeks glowed. Did the moon make him look like that?

"Will you again?"

"Never," she said. But then she thought better of it and said, "At least not exactly in the same way."

Somvay reached for the gun. Wary, she swung it behind her.

"Are you still drunk?"

He didn't answer, but his arm was steady.

"Nononono," Luke crooned. Severa checked him from the corner of her eye. Pat was flat out, maybe asleep, maybe something deeper. Luke brushed off a stripe of sand stuck to his brother's head. He kissed his brother's nose. Then he stopped and glared at her.

"You better shoot me fast," he said. "You better."

"Don't listen," she said, turning to Somvay. "Tell me more stuff."

"I'm done," he said, palm out.

The gun stayed in the small of her back. "Are you a monk? Were you before you came here?"

Behind her, she could hear Luke lurch to standing. "Who's a monk?"

"He is," Severa said, trying to change the air's flavor. "A monk," she repeated, like speaking the word could chill the scene.

Luke pushed past her and bellied up to Somvay. "If you're a monk, do something," he demanded. "Wake him up. Bring him back."

"I'm not magic." Somvay's voice was even. "I make meat."

A wet, horrible sound interrupted them. They all looked at flat Pat. Bubbles gushed past his teeth to his chin.

"Guy?" Luke pleaded with Somvay. "Any prayer you can say?"

But Somvay was silent. He relaxed his shoulders and let his head fall. Then Severa felt her arm jerk wildly in its socket, spinning her around as Luke stripped the gun. He pointed the gun at his face. Then he took dead aim at her.

"You got warned," Luke said, shaky. "Didn't you?"

Beside her, Somvay dropped to his knees. Severa shut her

eyes and waited for the world to break. One more second and it breaks.

Run, whispered someone.

So she ran. Through mud and pale-barked trees. She heard three shots, each ringing the same truth to her: *It's not me. It's not me. It's not me.*

SMART LIFE

Once life had been all about learning. Like last year, when her bio class studied death. They hit a mortuary and watched an autopsy in the hospital's polar basement morgue. Back at school, they grabbed live frogs out of buckets, poking needles into their sorry brains. Cats next—first dissected, then boiled so she and the rest of the kids could memorize bones.

Those days were gone. Now Severa sprawled on the mortuary's stiff gorgeous lawn, ripping through the *Register,* searching for names. In her pocket she had $29, not enough to let her cut town. And no doubt she had to leave. That morning, in the park, waking under a stand of stripped pines, legs barked with mud, the truth broke Severa like an ax would. She had to get out now.

Lila Lamereaux. Next to a soft-focus photo of a woman with loose skin and a brood of survivors including six grandkids.

Severa threw down the paper and checked her reflection in the bottom of a Coke can. Not too bad. She was three days dirty, but earlier she'd stuck her head under a sink in the park's public restroom and stopped by the Walgreen's to spray on tester perfume.

So go! She straightened herself and started walking, kicks poking holes in the lawn. From what she remembered, right inside the mortuary was a lobby, and beyond that a dinky chapel that smelled like fruit. Visitation happened in a series of dim woody chambers. On the field trip, the undertaker had led the class beyond them, to the embalming room, where he'd showed off two special lipped tables designed to catch cadaver goo.

As soon as Severa pushed into the building, a woman with a face as plain as butter appeared out of nowhere and immediately asked for a name.

"Lamereaux," Severa said.

"Oh," the woman said, smoothing her ebony suit, "I can't tell you how sorry I am, but visitation won't begin for, let's see, I guess it'll be another hour."

"I came early in the hope I could enjoy a private moment with my grandmom."

"A granddaughter?" The woman viewed her skeptically.

"We had the same initials, my grandmom and me." Was the woman's mouth getting softer? "When I was a child she used to take me camping. We would bring no food whatsoever. We'd hunt squirrels instead. When I saw a squirrel I'd throw a rock just past him, to scare him back in the direction of me. Then Grandmom would drop him with her gun."

The woman regarded her. "Squirrels are awfully tough eating, aren't they?"

"No," Severa said, sighing, like the precious memory pained her. "No, not if you cook them with milk and sage."

The woman hesitated, then reached for Severa's arm. She stopped when she saw it bandaged, wrist to elbow.

"Softball," Severa explained, offering the other one. "Slid for home."

At the chamber door, the woman motioned to an open guest book where Severa signed *Lola Lamereaux*. The woman walked her to a vaulted coffin probably ten times bigger than the little thing inside.

Severa gripped the box's velvet rim, not quite ready. Then she reminded herself how to look at something dead. Focus on one bit—remember?—not the whole. Like the tip of her dad's bit-off tongue, on the bedroom floor, gray as a tiny spoiled fish.

She sucked in some air and bent over. The woman backed off, and Severa waited until she sensed her disappear. Even then, if somebody were watching, it would look like Severa was holding her grandmom's hand, or fixing her hair, or adjusting the collar of her wrap dress printed paisley pink.

But in reality, she was checking fingers for rings and ears for diamonds. And around Grandmom's throat, all the checking paid off: a triple-strand choker of pearls!

Severa leaned closer. She speed-chanted a mantra, to maybe move this lady up the bardo chain. Then she unfixed the choker and, in a voice loud enough to reach anyone, said, "Please watch over those of us still down here."

In the bus, stuck next to a guy picking his toes, Severa thought about how the five senses failed. Like if you hear a shot, but don't see it, all you really know is that a bullet escaped its gun. The sixth sense—clairvoyance—now that was different. Knowledge couldn't be fucked with coming through the mind's eye.

"Keep going," she warned the toe-picker, "you'll hit bone." Then she shoved past him to jump off the bus. She walked Sixth Avenue to the pawn shop she'd used before. There, a long shirtless boy in a white baseball cap sat on the stoop, smoking and strumming his abs. Super. The shop wasn't open yet. Severa sat on the step beneath the boy and arranged her legs so her good muscles showed.

"Looks like you're thinking hard," she said, faking awe.

The boy withdrew his cigarette and stared at the burning end like it was gold. "Yeah," he said, "my mind's near to full." Beside him was a freezer bag filled with scratched-up plastic Smurfs. He eyed them. "How much you think they'll give me for these?"

"I wouldn't give you a dollar."

The boy frowned. "I don't know," he said. "People like toys."

He offered her a cigarette from a close-to-empty pack. She lit hers off his and then cased him. Threadbare old school Vans. Cut-off Levis. The letters U-BET sewn into his cap.

"U-BET?" she asked.

"Us Being Entrepreneurial Together. Like friendship in business and business in friendship."

"And you sell what?"

"Magazine subscriptions." He stopped smoking for a second to cough. "I answered this ad back in Madison for 'bright boys who want to see our nation firsthand!' It said, 'Plenty of dough and good times!'"

Severa shot him a smile, grateful to meet somebody so green. All signs were that he was as soft as bread, and let's face it, those are the best guys to hang around.

"How long you in town?" she asked.

"We pull out tomorrow night, but first, tomorrow day, we go to the mall. That's why I'm pawning these."

"Where's your plenty of dough?"

"It's complicated. On the one hand is what they owe you, and on the other is what you owe them. And the magazines have to get their bite." The boy shrugged. "But hey, I get to see the country, shore to shore." He dragged on his cigarette. "Most mornings there's donuts besides."

They heard the lock turn and turn back from inside the shop. When they looked, a little man in an orange smock shook his head and mouthed, *Not today,* before pulling the shade.

The boy sighed. "Maybe Senior will advance me more cash."

"He's your boss?" asked Severa, always thinking. "He's got plenty of dough?" When the boy nodded, her heart speeded up. She might be able to score some scratch, or at least a lift out of town. "Think I could meet him?" she said.

The boy's expression turned cagey. "There's no girls on the U-BET team."

"Look," she said, deciding to try another way, "I don't want to weird you. But sometimes I get a feeling about people, and I think I got one now." She moved close enough to rub her hair against his chin. "Fact is I'd love to give us a chance," she said. "To be entrepreneurial. Together."

The boy flushed and said, "I'm not supposed to like girls."

"That's cool," she reassured him. "Me and you both."

Severa followed the boy, whose name was Troy, to where the U-BET team was staying, a flaking ranch-style motel built around a pool. He led her to a small room where a dozen skinny boys in blue U-BET sweatshirts lounged on two queen beds, eating bear claws and drinking light ice beer. In the corner, on the room's solo chair, sat an old man. His face was like a rock that had rolled down a mountain—chipped up, but still mostly whole. Under his red U-BET cap, his color was bad.

"Who do we have?" the old man asked, in a voice surprisingly strong.

"Senior, this is Lola," Troy said. "I met her in town."

When Senior focused, Severa saw his eyes were little pondlets of fire. The U-BET boys rearranged themselves, crowding onto one bed, so she could sit on the other next to Senior's chair. She was gearing up to have a go at him, but before she could, the old man started on her.

"You done something bad. What's up, sister?"

"I ain't done shit," she said, a little freaked he could tell.

"I can see it all over you. You are far from clean."

"So wash me, big boy." She twitted her lashes. "Is that what you wanted to hear?"

He chuckled low. "How old are you? Fifteen? Sixteen?"

"I'm an ageless creature!" she said, letting her voice go shrieky. "I'm no age at all!"

"Oh my." He smiled, fingers fluttering on his knee. "By the way, you needn't keep an eye on my hand," he said. "I don't touch."

Hold it. In her mind, Severa stepped back to check the scene. She didn't want to offer to sell the necklace in front of the boys, now glued to MTV. They might be dumb, but she was outnumbered, and she couldn't be sure they wouldn't grab the pearls. Besides, maybe she could get something for nothing. She lifted her messed-up arm for Senior to see.

"Look," she said, starting over. "I'm trying to escape from a bad home. Troy told me you're super kind. Maybe you have cash to spare?"

Senior pointed at her. "You did that to yourself. I don't know how, but the bulk of your misery is self-inflicted, that's for certain." He patted his face idly. "But someday, perhaps, I might buy you a beer. I can see you're good at what you do. That I admire."

"I got the skills to pay the bills," Severa purred, moving in. "And I do mean the skills."

He laughed at her again. "You can't dirty-talk me, sister. You don't need to. You want to go on a ride, it's simple: ask me. We'll go."

"Where we headed?"

"Oh, someplace different. Someplace you've never been."

"I can see you're real stupid. There's no place different. It's all like right here."

"I have to admit," Senior said slowly, "you do have a very slight sour charm. And for that, as a reward, I'll impart a secret to you. Are you ready?"

"Let me have it," Severa said.

"My life," he began, "is a journey about discovering that I'm not as terrible as I originally thought. If you want, your life could be about that too."

"What do I care about finding out if you're terrible?"

"If you're terrible," he corrected her.

"That's what I said. What's the point?" In the last few hours she'd snatched pearls from a dead lady's throat. Look back further, she'd done worse. Her whole enterprise now was motion only, running faster than whatever was behind her. Until the day came—and she knew it would—when she'd trip over herself and wipe out.

Shut in the van, Severa could smell herself, funky as cat food. She needed a bath really bad. Still, the team seemed to like her. They let her sit shotgun, squeezing themselves in back. The morning beer had blown a goodwill bubble big enough for them all.

Senior dropped the team at one end of Foster Drive. The neighborhood was way too nice for people to buy magazines from a kid at their door, but Severa didn't tell. She had to admire the whole operation, stringing boys along with donuts and the delusion they were having fun. She stayed in the van and watched the team fan out. Meanwhile, Senior kept the engine running, so they could beat it fast if need be.

"So how's the sales rap go?" she asked him.

He didn't take his pouchy eyes off the team. "Depends on who answers the door. If it's a chic type of lady, you might say part of the money will be donated to a woman's shelter. Or if it's a man, you can say it's for crippled kids."

"But in truth the money goes straight to you?"

"I have big pockets," he said mildly. "Something needs to fill them."

"And how come there aren't any girls?"

"I can rely on boys. They're loyal."

"Girls aren't?" she asked, like the idea hadn't occurred to her, like she didn't believe it was true.

"I've given this a lot of thought," he said. "There's men and there's women. I am a man. These boys are men. And a man is what you might call a captain, a protector of honor and what's right. What I mean is: a man goes down with his ship."

"Uh-huh," she said.

"Then you have women. Not captains, correct? Ladies are more like—if you have to label them—stewardesses. And do you know what stewardesses are trained to do? If the fire gets too hot, or the smoke's too thick, or the water's too deep, get off that plane any way you can. Save yourself first."

She studied him. There was something about people who came up with ways to cut the world into pieces, however wrong their systems might be.

"You're telling me some day all the men will be underwater while I'm up here working it unburned and alive?" she said.

Senior didn't respond. A minivan had turned onto the street, its white hood painted NEIGHBORHOOD WATCH. He gave the horn two quick beeps. At the sound, boys in driveways ducked into bushes or behind people's cars. Troy, at someone's door, tried to step inside.

The minivan crept the length of the street. Senior gripped the steering wheel. After the car turned, he honked three times, and the team made a mad run for the van.

"We got some complaints yesterday out in Glen Oaks," Senior explained. "I'm trying to keep our profile low."

The team bundled in, cursing Des Moines and fat rent-a-cops. No sales meant no commissions, and the vibe, in the van, was real glum. Severa listened, eyes shut, lost in the high buzz of their bitching. She pictured herself somewhere else, in some loud market, where guys hustled rice and brown fruit.

The team wanted her to tour them around the city, but Severa totally declined. Too many places to avoid. The Lost Planet, for obvious reasons. And after leaving Doug's crib, she didn't want to show her face there. Then there was the wee garden apartment in which her dad had died. It had been hers for the last three weeks, but she couldn't stand to be where she'd found him hanging, blue and pop-eyed. Where the truth had nailed her that he didn't love her at all.

So they returned, restless, to the motel. At the back of the room was a sliding glass door that opened to a stretch of fake grass and the pool. Troy cracked it and allowed in a weak breeze. Severa took to the closet to change into somebody's T-shirt and boxers. In the bathroom Senior used the tub to mix Everclear with Kool-Aid.

After everyone filled their glasses, Severa followed the boys outside. The pool was small, but got deep in the middle. She stood on the lip so the underwater spots could light her legs.

"I'd like to propose a toast," Senior said, brandishing an ice bucket of punch. "An old Cheyenne proverb." He cleared his throat. "A nation is not lost so long as its women's hearts are high. But if ever the woman's heart should be lost, then the nation dies." He raised the bucket, and the boys lifted their own cups. "To Lola!"

Severa accepted the toast with a desultory wave, then chug-chugged her punch. She wanted to swim. But first, her screwed arm. She unwrapped the bandages slowly, wincing at air on skin. Lines of thick black stitches crossed her arms at angles. Smaller scratches budded red. This girl needed chlorine!

She dove in, and right off was skinny and stronger, held no more by that planetary pull. No noseplugs, but she did her synchro moves anyway: a decent oyster that morphed into a barracuda that turned into a double ballet leg as she sculled the pool's length. Legs bent at the knees, she whipped around a few flamingo turns, then tipped back and let herself sink. Water shot her sinuses. Her eyes burned. She curled to a ball and drifted to the bottom, then pushed off and broke the surface again.

The boys screamed with applause.

Hearing them, Severa wondered where the other guests were. Maybe hiding in their rooms, too scared to complain. Or maybe there were no other guests. Maybe beyond this motel, some big thing was happening, and the city had emptied itself out. Or maybe at last she'd remade Des Moines into a place that pleased her: full of dumb boys, herself at the center, cold and near naked and clean.

Man, was she fucked up. Head spinning, she lifted herself out of the pool. Somebody gave her a towel and a glass of red punch. She walked the length of the diving board and struck a pose.

"I have a toast," she said.

Everybody waited.

"This moon," she said, flinging an arm to the daytime sky. "This taste in my mouth, this life. All of it mind. All mind."

She drank the punch fast as they clapped and clapped.

Later, both squeezed into a pool chair, Troy told Severa about a girl who gave birth to a thirteen-pound baby with a tooth. Severa liked the story, but not when Troy felt her up.

"Come on," he urged. "Now you touch my boob."

Everything confused her. Like how the ground seemed infinite, and the sky was a dark rock-solid lump. She obligingly pawed Troy, but focused on a tale Senior was telling boys by the diving board, about seeing a Frenchman thrown through the window of a titty bar in New Orleans. The Frenchman stood, blood roping off him, and cried, "Merci!" before he collapsed and got hit by a car.

Senior raised his glass to her. "Merci!" he called.

"Where's the blood?" she asked.

"Where's the car?" Troy said to her neck.

"Where's the titties?" said one of the boys.

Senior pushed the boy into the pool. Severa drank to him and to the story of the crazy Frenchman who—at first—survived. Then she pictured herself in the van's front seat beside Senior. The country passing by like a filmstrip. Boys handing her cash, her dishing donuts like a queen.

So she made sure to ask Senior—before she stumbled into a room, before she fell onto her first bed in three nights, before her dream body rose from her real body to tiptoe around a higher plane—if the next day she could join the team.

Waking alone on the bed, boys sprawled on the floor around her, Severa realized that her arm felt OK. Truly it wasn't as bad as before.

She stepped off the bed and over boys. In someone's duffel she found a U-BET tank top she could wear like a dress. She'd hidden her own bag in the top shelf of the closet, and now she pulled her dad's copy of the *Dhammapada* from inside. Missing, of course, the page he'd pinned to his chest, like a kid with a note sent home from school.

At the bottom of her bag, Severa found the choker. She hooked the pearls around her neck, shoved back her bag, and left the room.

A folded *Des Moines Register* waited for Senior outside his door. She kicked it aside and went in. The sight of him scared her at first. Asleep he could pass for newly dead. But he rose quick when she asked him to drive her somewhere before the boys woke up and wanted to ride along.

In the van, she directed him to Waveland Cemetery. He made a beautiful turn under its scrolled iron gate.

"Nice necklace," he said, parking by the sales office.

"Fake."

"Sure," he said, slight-smiling. "Good. Keep a secret. Never tell the whole truth."

Severa ran ahead while Senior searched in the van for a towel. After a hot wet summer, her dad's marker already looked overgrown. She pulled weeds and wiped away mud until she could see everything clearly: his name and dates and, carved above them, in dark letters, GONE BEFORE. Severa sat on the grass and opened her dad's *Dhammapada.* If she didn't get him out of the first bardo soon, his soul would never leave her alone. But before she could start, Senior appeared, puffing, towel in hand.

"Who's this joker?" he said.

"My dad."

"A dead dad." He used the towel to blot his face. "How'd he die?"

"Hung himself."

Senior shook his head. "Some people lack the long view."

"I guess he didn't have your brilliant secret. About the find-out-you're-not-terrible trip." She squinted at him. "How's that work anyway?"

Senior spread the towel beside the grave. He lowered himself to it, joints resisting, then reclined until his head rested on stone.

"You run into people much worse," he said.

Severa let the book close. "That makes you feel better?"

"I feel great."

She looked at Senior's face. Reclined, his skin hung back, making him look one century old instead of two.

"Something you said last night," he said, "it's my favorite thing I've heard all year." He offered his hand and for some reason she took it, his palm like a worn paper bag.

"I translated it to Spanish," he said. "Todo es mío."

She tried to bring back hours of language class. "All is mine?"

His eyes were closed now. His fingers moved in hers. "Todo es mío. Todo es mío, todo es mío."

"I said, 'All is mind,'" she informed him. "Mind."

"Todo es mío. Ésta luna, éste gusto en mi boca, ésta vida." His voice was deep and scary and almost enough.

"Todo es mía," she said.

"Todo es mío!" Senior's mouth opened wide and then wider. "Mi cuerpo, mi cerebro, mi corazón . . ."

The sun low in the sky meant not much color in anything. Severa dropped Senior's hand and breathed slower, checking vibes. She felt nothing. That's good, she told herself. Everyone—she hoped—had moved on.

Back at the hotel, the boys were awake and waiting, sitting on the beds half-dressed and dull-eyed.

"We're hungry," one of the smaller ones intoned.

Troy beheld Severa coolly. "Yeah," he said.

"Donut run," Senior announced. "I'll be back with the goods." He rushed out the door before Severa could join him. As soon as he left, Troy approached and sniffed her neck.

"Hella nice jewels," he said,

She'd forgotten she was sporting the pearls. "Hey," she said, breezy. "I'm off to Senior's room. I need a hot shower."

"It's locked," Troy said.

"You have a key?"

"I don't know about keys," Troy said. "But I got something else." He snapped his fingers, and a boy stepped forward, with a *Register* unrolled.

THREE FOUND DEAD AT "LOST PLANET." A photo of the lime pit and three bodies under sheets. Severa's chest went tight and achy.

"We found some things in the closet," Troy said, holding up Somvay's credit card and photo. "We added two to two."

"I didn't even think you fellas could read," she said. "Much less do math."

"You done something bad, Lola." Troy was sorrowful. "You killed junkies and then tried to cover it up." He read from the paper. "'According to police, the men were involved in a methamphetamine deal gone awry. But the sister of one of the victims, Somvay Khamvongsa, disputed the official account. 'My brother was not a drug user,' Onesy Khamvongsa told reporters. 'He was a good man.'" Troy glanced up. "Says here cops declined to comment on her claims."

"It's a long story," Severa managed to say, though her throat was closing. "I'm gross. Give me the key."

Troy removed one from his pocket and dropped it on the floor. When she bent to it, someone behind her growled.

"My grandma would call that a naughty bottom," Troy said.

"My grandmom's dead," Severa said quickly. "She just died."

"Do you miss her?"

"Yeah," Severa said. "I truly do."

"Would you like to talk to her? I mean, if we knew how to make that happen?"

"SÉANCE," the team said then, in one dark voice.

The room's air conditioning struggled on, though the room was freezing. Severa knew the team wanted her to resist, to get the situation interesting. But she wasn't going to make things harder than they had to be.

She stretched on the bed, and the boys circled around her. Troy produced a black bandana to tie over her eyes. Each of the boys worked two fingers under her. "Light as a feather," they chanted. "Stiff as a board."

Hard to tell if energy was entering or draining from her, but either way she rose off the bed. As she went higher, her body got heavier. The blindfold failed—she saw all sorts of things. A bowl with a fistful of rice in it. The deck of a boat, slick with the guts of fish.

Then she saw herself running away from the Lost Planet, lurching in her fuck-me kicks.

So when she felt fingers undoing the pearls, she didn't say anything. Nothing when they dropped her on the bed. They left the blindfold tied, but still she was quiet, as they cracked the sliding door and launched themselves, boy by boy, into the pool.

But one boy stayed bedside, dipping over her. His breath caught in the wet of his nose.

"If you could be anyone," Severa whispered, "who would you be?"

"Not you," said Troy.

Tiny clicks and pinches followed, but not until he started

pulling did she know what he'd done. Her stitches came out, impossibly slow. She coughed up something hot.

Troy stopped. He wiped her face with the sheet. Then he took her arm again.

At first it felt good. Or—at least—better. But soon the stinging started and her skin warmed with blood. Her arm wasn't hers. Nothing was.

"What do you say now?" Troy said. "Little Miss I'm-Number-One?"

"Thank you," Severa choked. Then, in a dream, she was on a plane that flew into the ocean. Things got dark and then darker, cold and then colder, until finally she crashed into the sea floor.

Somebody slapped her as she moved toward a massive glass wall.

"I'm your father," a voice said, "and we're not from here, we're driving through, with no insurance, and at a rest stop a feral cat attacked your arm."

Severa remembered. "Where's Troy?" she asked.

Senior shoved her, and she fell off the hospital's sidewalk and landed in a plot of pink plants. Her arm was wrapped in a thin hotel towel and someone had slipped on her kicks.

"The team showed me an interesting article on this morning's front page," Senior said from above her. He spoke easily, like they were in the grocery store, waiting together in a long line to pay. "Seems your enlightened Chamber of Commerce has a new city slogan."

It confused her. What did he know?

"Say goodbye to *Des Moines: The Surprising Place.* From now on, it's *Des Moines: Smart Life.*"

Where did all my powers go? she wondered. Do old people get bored this fast?

"My first reaction: what's so damn smart about it?" Senior tried to kneel, but his bad knees stopped him. "Then I thought more, and the slogan seemed truer. You got to be smart to stay alive. Here or anywhere." He stretched out a hand. "Be smart, Lola. Let's not lose you too."

Inside the emergency room, a lady doctor hung over the reception desk, chatting up a ripped male nurse. Severa recognized her from three nights before—neat little fingers, clunky rubber clogs.

The doctor eyed her. "I got this one," she told the nurse. And to Senior, "Sir, you wait here."

Senior tried to protest, but the doctor ignored him, leading Severa down the hall. When she looked back, he was watching her, maybe fondly. Then he pulled the pearl choker from his pocket. He bit the pearls, checking the grit with his teeth.

The doctor closed a set of curtains that had gone gray from washing. Severa sat on a loud paper-lined cot.

"So?" the doctor asked. "Another window disrespect you?"

"I cut the stitches myself," Severa said. "They were ugly. Then things got a little out of control."

"And that old man? He's not the kid who brought you in last time."

"I'm lucky," she said. "Guardian angels? I have tons."

The doctor swabbed her arm aggressively, not buying her crap. "No one has the right to abuse you."

"Except me," Severa pointed out. "I mean, that's allowed."

The doctor gave up. She worked fast, cleaning and wrapping, fastening a new bandage with metal pins. "Don't protect anybody," she said. "Try to remember who the victim is."

Have you ever killed someone? Severa should have asked her. Did a procedure ever go wrong in the middle? How do you stand working here?

But it was too late for questions. The doctor left, and Severa returned to the waiting room, fixed arm pulsating at her side. She looked for Senior but didn't see him. She checked the turnaround, and the chapel, then circled the lobby, ending at the men's restroom.

"Senior?" she called, pushing open the door.

A little kid on his way out asked if she'd lost her dog.

Outside the hospital, in the drive where the ambulances rolled in, Severa parked herself on the curb. Why was she surprised U-BET had moved on to the next place, hawking magazines that would never arrive?

"I told them it wasn't nice to leave you," Senior said.

He was beside her. Right there. She tried to keep the relief from her face, but it showed up anyway. She watched him make note.

"Was that before or after you ditched me?"

Senior shrugged, smiling, and handed her an open beer.

Yeah, she thought, taking it, why wouldn't he be happy? The truth was finally out. He could leave anytime he wanted to, and all she'd be was grateful if he returned.

"So where do we stand?" he asked. "Did you keep your secret?"

She drank from the can before answering. "Did you keep yours?"

"Yes," he said. "For now, you're the one secret I'm keeping." He took the beer back. "You make me feel good."

The U-BET team was waiting around the corner with the van. Troy wore a fresh T-shirt printed with a chest X-ray. He handed her a box of candy, a half-pound.

"What's this?" she asked.

"Hospital gift shop." He displayed Somvay's credit card before slapping it into Senior's palm. "People here trust anybody. Seriously—do I look like a Somvay?"

Senior cracked open the van door. In a rush, the boys scrambled for seats. Once they were in, he locked the door, before disappearing to the driver's side.

For a second, Severa lingered on the grass. It's not like she didn't see how it was. She knew if she got in that van anything she might find there would be short-term and come with strings attached. But if there was anything for her out here, she sure couldn't find it. So fuck it, she was going inside.

"Good job," Senior said as she climbed in. He fastened her seat belt, though he never wore his.

Then it dawned on her. "If I make you feel good," she asked, "does that mean you think I'm worse than you?"

"Congratulations," Senior said, speeding toward I-80. "You've finally seen the light."

Senior's knees by his ears and his ears bleeding on them. Fingers tight on the steering wheel, jammed under his chin. Cheek sliced deep, down to the fat, yellow and curdy as eggs.

Severa unbuckled herself and moved to him. She cupped his mouth and nose to feel for air. Thumb between his lips, she felt loose teeth. His tongue, when she touched, was still warm.

In back, the boys had been thrown into a pile, mouths open and limbs bent completely wrong. Severa leaned out her window and puked. Head hanging, she saw how a low wire fence kept the van from tipping to the field below.

The pearl choker was in Senior's pocket. She took it, then unwedged his wallet from his pants. She took a couple twenties and Somvay's photo, but left the credit card for the cops to find.

Who's the smart one now? she whispered. Of course no one answered, and then she felt bad for asking.

She dumped the candy Troy had given her and stuffed everything in the empty box. Then she slid out the window, over the fence. From the field, the road was invisible. But she could hear sirens, blaring weak against the sky.

She crawled into the cornstalks and followed their dry paths for a while, before hiking back up to the road. In the distance, the cops worked the crash scene. One swung a crowbar. Another knelt in the road, lighting flares. Severa walked faster. Her kicks had disappeared in the accident, and the asphalt cut her feet, but if she kept going, she'd get used to it soon.

Trucks speeding by her made the road shake. She was limping when a car finally stopped. Two boys were inside: the square one driving and, in back, a kid with red hair.

"U-BET," said the driver. "Where you headed?"

She tried to think. What was the next state? Some boring place without hills?

"Where you going?" she asked him.

"Denver. We have a youth conference there."

"I can go that way," she said. The red-haired boy pushed open his door. She moved next to him, candy box in her lap.

Youth conference was a clue, but it wasn't until she smelled them—pecans, white flowers, soap—that she knew.

"Why'd you all pick me up?" she asked.

The boy next to her grinned. "You seemed in need of a ride."

She shook her head. "You're good kids, aren't you?"

"We're Catholic," the driver said, "if that's what you mean."

"That's not what I mean." Then she was shaking like crazy. The red-haired boy took off his sweater and helped her into it, fitting the sleeve over her poor arm.

The sweater was scratchy. The sweater warmed her. That stupid sweater unfroze her little mind. EMPTY THE BOAT OF YOUR LIFE, her dad's last note had instructed. WHEN EMPTY IT SWIFTLY SAILS. Now she saw how she'd misread it, like your life was the thing to throw off the boat. When really the boat and your life were the same.

"Stop," she said. Nothing happened, so she screamed it: "STOP!"

Scared, the driver slammed the brakes, and the car skidded, tires on fire. When it was over, they were safe on the shoulder. A smell like old shoes dangled in the air. Severa checked to make sure she had everything. Somvay's photo—to return to his family and to back up her confession. Pearls—for counting the mantras that might free everyone from being born again.

"What happened?" the driver asked, dazed.

But she was already gone, running back, the weight of herself on her feet.

THE SURPRISING PLACE

But what if Green doesn't die? What if he wakes up in the hospital, pinned to his bed by a sandbag, the wall TV glowing bright?

Onscreen, a topless woman is side-lying, one arm thrown over her head like she's modeling for art. A diapered baby wiggles at her breast, and this baby is the whitest one Green has ever seen. A ghost baby, to tell the truth. But the kid has some fight. He jabs at his mother with his miniature fist, then settles into the feeding. Cut to a close-up of his pursed, sucking lips.

Green's fingertips itch, his mouth tastes of chalk, and there's something in his nose. When he turns from the TV to the window, he can sense the weight on top of him slowly shifting, and beneath it, a deep, pointed pain. Dr. Cureg explained the procedure to him: a stent inserted into a blood vessel near his groin and then guided to his gummed-up heart. But as far as Green can remember, a sandbag wasn't involved.

What Green does remember is standing in the snow, a strange woman in his arms, and then feeling like a seed in his chest suddenly blasted into bud. After that came the ambulance, a dose of strong medicine, then hum and fuzz until the bedside conference with Cureg explaining the plan. Green signed papers in yellow and pink and white triplicate, accepting all risks. Nora's eyes glinted, but she didn't cry.

A nurse in unicorn scrubs walks into the room. She glances at the TV, where the breastfeeding woman is switching holds. The woman, sitting, bolstered by a bank of pillows, balances the baby on her forearm and eases her nipple into his mouth. The nurse frowns.

"That channel," she says, "is for new mothers." Then she starts on Green's vitals, clipping a pincher to his finger and wrapping a blood pressure gauge around his upper arm. She revs up her machine, and Green can feel his neck throb as the cuff compresses, pauses at its tightest point, and ticks its slow release. The long wait unnerves him, recalling a childhood game in which his father grabbed Green's finger and squeezed. "If you don't try to get away," his father said, "I'll let go." Then, in unbearable increments, his father loosened his hold. To Green, it seemed an eternity until his father might free him, so as soon as his father's fist began to relax, he tried to yank his finger away. But his father always caught him, tightening his grip before Green could escape. "Now we start over," his father would sigh.

The nurse taps her nails on the machine until red numbers appear. She writes them down, then unclips the pincher and removes the cuff.

"Can you tell me what the sandbag is for?" Green asks.

"Heavy post-op bleeding at the entry site. The weight encourages clotting."

"How long do I have to have it on?"

"Until the bleeding stops."

"Has it stopped?"

"I'd have to take off the bag to check."

Green waits.

"How's your pain?" The nurse produces a laminated strip featuring a continuum of hand-drawn faces, with cartoonish expressions ranging from *Yippee!* to *I-Can't-Take-No-More.* Green points to a face in the middle, its mouth a straight line.

"All right," the nurse says. She pulls a brown container from her pocket and offers Green two pills and a sip of water from a straw cup. "Now that you're awake, I'll send your family in."

Green experiences his first flicker of panic.

"Don't worry," the nurse says. "You look fine." She pats his arm before she goes.

Green's sweaty, not even sure what's inside him. He tries to picture the stent tunneling his artery, keeping plaque at bay. Instead, he gets a vision of an untended garden. He thinks of how nature eventually overtakes design.

The door to his room swings wide.

"I told her you'd make it," says Roy as he enters. He's in an army jacket, right sleeve loose.

"You're back!" Nora exclaims, voice high in her throat. She gives Green a tight-mouthed kiss that tastes like vanilla.

"Mmm," he says.

"They have free coffee by the Neuro ICU. With flavors!"

"She's high as a kite," Roy says.

Nora exhales and her lashes flutter. "It's been a long day."

"You want to lie down?" Green asks.

She cocks her head like she's considering it, and Green tries to scoot over, so she won't think too long. But the sandbag slows him.

"Don't," Nora says. She arranges herself on the edge of the bed, tilting her body, resting her purse on her hip. Once balanced, she sets her cheek on Green's shoulder, and it's the closest they've been in a while. He steadies his breath, so as not to spook her.

"Hey," Roy says. "What about me?"

Green gestures to the sandbag, meaning, *No room.* But Roy misunderstands the message. He wedges his arm under the sandbag, lifts, and drops the bag on the floor.

The sudden air on Green's skin makes him shiver. Looking down, he sees a thatch of taped gauze, and how he's bled through it, though the blood has since dried. Then he realizes he's exposed.

"Thanks," he says, quickly replacing his sheet.

"What's left is strong," Roy says. "Now make way."

Green hesitates, then angles toward Nora. He feels a pull somewhere, but it's not too bad. Nora hooks her leg over his and slides her head to his chest.

"Is this OK?" she asks. "Does it hurt?"

"I'm fine," Green says and means it.

Roy maneuvers his knee brace as he stretches onto the bed. The absence of his arm brings him right next to Green on the pillow, ear to ear.

"What are we watching?" he asks.

On TV, the topless woman is smoothing lanolin onto her aureoles, the baby nowhere to be seen. Green's flooded with warmth, and then a series of commands flows to him: *Hang yourself like a coat. Sink yourself like a nail. Step into yourself like a pool.*

"So I've come up with a plan!" Nora says. "I'm going to go to law school. I'll take night classes after work."

Her ambition startles him. "A full day at the high school and more school at night?"

Against his chest, he feels Nora's jaw shift. "You haven't been paying attention," she says. "There's nothing I can't do."

"Superwoman," agrees Roy.

"I guess I should have a heart attack more often," Green suggests. "It fires you up."

"Speaking of Superwoman," Roy says to Nora, "have a baby too, while you're at it." He points to the TV. "Green will stay home. He knows how to nurse."

"I'm serious." Nora lifts her chin to regard Green, her gaze flinty. "I thought there was time to get it together. But this is it. You're either in or you're out."

"Be on," Roy declares, "or be off."

Normally it bothers Green when they gang up on him, talking in code he doesn't know how to break. But not today. He'll take it today. Today he'll lie cozy and quiet between them, pondering the ceiling, its blank expanse almost as good as sky.

"My man is tripping," Roy says.

"Hold on." Nora reaches into her bag and retrieves a glassine envelope like the ones his father used to preserve First Day Covers. "I found this when I was looking for insurance," she says, giving it to Green. "Your mother was going to throw it out when they moved, but I stopped her."

The envelope's filled with white pebbles. No—with baby teeth.

"Are those all his?" Roy asks, awed. "Or are some mine?"

Green lifts the flap and spills teeth onto his palm, until it appears he's cupping a small mound of dried corn. He stares at the teeth, relics of a smaller self. Then Roy pinches a tooth, raises it to his lips, and grins.

Green's head gets lighter. The enormous difference between what's inside and outside of his brother is too much. His eyes tear.

"See?" Nora says, and it sounds like's she choked up too. "It goes fast."

Green looks up at the screen. The video must have looped to the beginning, because the ghost baby's back, and the topless woman has a shirt on, though she's already starting to unbutton it again.

If we finish the attic, Green thinks, it could be a good nursery. He has some antique flour bins salvaged from his grandfather's house that would work for toy storage, and he'd design built-ins for the baby's clothes. It's true they'd need to add another staircase climbing from the second floor, to meet code. But with two sets of stairs, he realizes, they'd be able to split the attic and use half as an office. Nora could study there, while the baby sleeps and he and Roy catch the Hawks on TV. At feeding time they'll bring her the baby, and be together, the four of them, below the eaves.

"Watch out," he hears his brother say. "There he goes."

It's a lot to keep straight at the moment, but with paper in front of him, Green knows he could sketch out a plan. For now, he feels Nora sweep the teeth from his palm. His body lifts as she and Roy rise from the bed. When the door to his room opens and closes again, it sounds like turning to a book's final page.

But it's not the end. Everything returns. Until then, Green will dream his new project, plotting its shape and scale.

How do I make it real?

JUNIPER

JUNIPER PRIZE FOR FICTION

This volume is the fifteenth recipient
of the Juniper Prize for Fiction,
established in 2004 by the
University of Massachusetts Press
in collaboration with the
UMass Amherst MFA Program
for Poets and Writers, to be
presented annually for an outstanding
work of literary fiction. Like its sister award,
the Juniper Prize for Poetry established
in 1976, the prize is named in honor
of Robert Francis (1901–1987),
who lived for many years at
Fort Juniper, Amherst, Massachusetts.